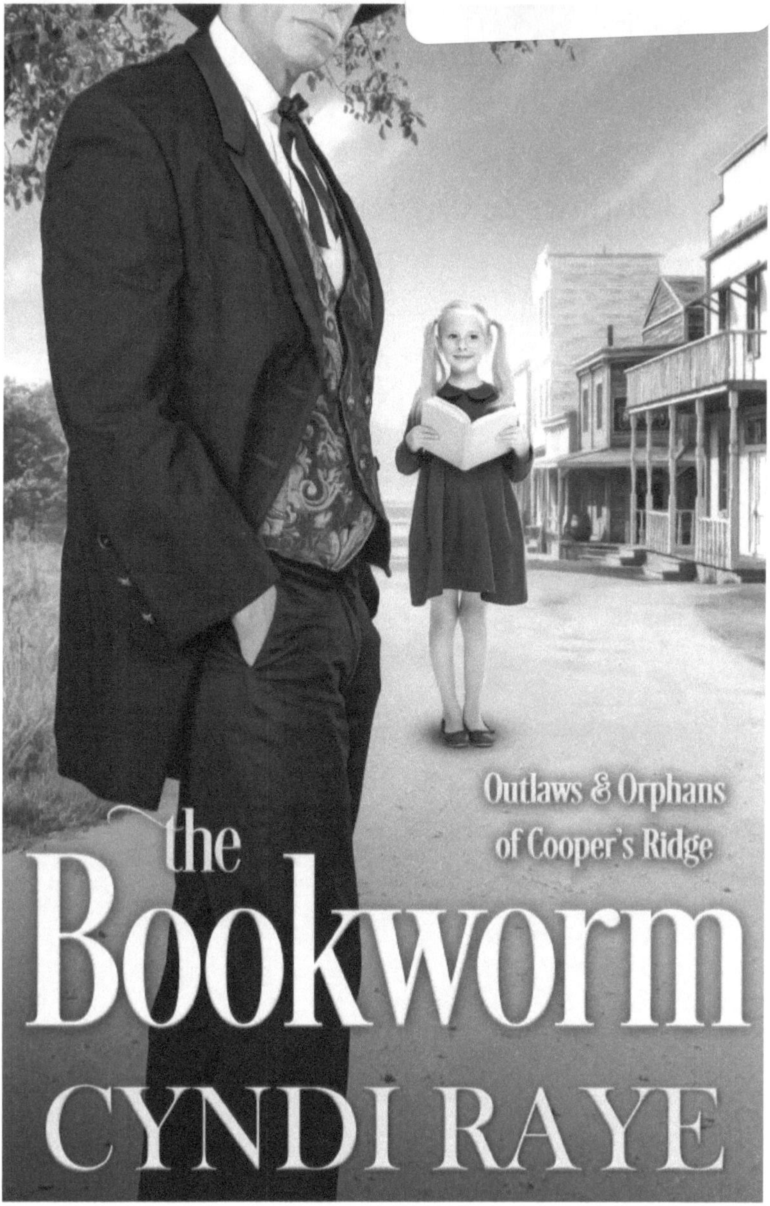
Outlaws & Orphans
of Cooper's Ridge
the
Bookworm
CYNDI RAYE

The Bookworm

Outlaws & Orphans of Cooper's Ridge
Book 4
by
CYNDI RAYE

---

1. http://www.CyndiRaye.com

Outlaws & Orphans of Cooper's Ridge is a spin-off from Cyndi Raye's **Sons of Nora White** series.

Cooper Murphy wore many badges in his outlaw days after the war. When he realizes he was becoming like the outlaws he chased, he returns home to change his life. Now a rough-speaking, gun toting man of God, he buys a plot of land and slowly builds the town of Cooper's Ridge. But there are rules and regulations to follow. Cooper's Ridge is for those who were once sinful and now have redeemed themselves, wanting to build a new life in a town that won't shame a man for his past behaviors. Can he keep peace and help build a town filled with character and redemption? Book 7 is Samantha 'Sam' Malone's story.

Don't forget to visit www.cyndiraye.com [1] for a free short story from Mail Order Brides of Wichita Falls series.

---

1. http://www.cyndiraye.com

Chapter 1

"Welcome to Sam's Book Shop." Sam took a deep breath and faced the crowd. She hadn't expected to be so nervous, but every single person she knew in town had walked through the front door when she opened it a few minutes ago. Now, it was time to introduce herself properly.

Everyone in town knew her as Sam, the woman who dressed in men's trousers and cowboy boots and worked at the livery. She had been living in the boarding house and working for Tom Hamilton, the livery owner since she left Noel, Kansas, at the end of last winter. Knowing she was opening a book store, they began to call her the Book Lady.

Her life was almost complete. She had worked hard these past months to make a home for herself and a business where she was in total control of her destiny. She had lived most of her life at St. Catherine's House of Sisterhood in New York City. When she had turned eighteen, she had been put out by the nuns, given money and her carpet bag and sent out into the streets to find her own way.

Except, she knew where she was going. She always had a plan.

It had been quite rough getting to this point in her life but looking around now, she was satisfied. Sam was now nearing the final stages of her planned journey. After this, there was only one more thing she had to face, but she still wasn't ready for that yet.

She fingered the gold chain with a small locket around her neck, then tucked it back inside her neckline where she kept it hidden most of the time. Maybe soon. She wasn't sure.

Sam gave the crowd a huge smile. "You all know me as Sam, the pants-wearing stable hand. My real name is Samantha Rebecca Angelina Corta Allena Malone." She curtsied in her new skirt and blouse, then shifted from one foot to the other. These ballerina shoes were hideous and she was going to change her shoes as soon as she was able. Sam had a new pair of kid boots that she had purchased when she bought the dress the other day.

Knowing she had to present herself as more of a professional if she wanted to be a successful business woman and be taken seriously, Sam had given herself the gift of a new wardrobe. She now had a few skirts, blouses and dresses to wear during shop hours. It wasn't that she'd never dress in men's britches again, but she had to be taken seriously in order to earn a good living for herself. From the looks of most of the townsfolk, they all needed her books.

"Who in the world gave you a name like that?" One of the men in the crowd called out. He was one of the regular men who was always heckling in church, too.

"Hush up and wait for me to explain things," she told the man. "I may have a new dress and my own business, but you best act proper in my store or I'll have you thrown out lickety-split!"

"I believe her!" Another one of the usual hecklers spoke above the smiling faces of the crowd. "Go on now, tell us how you got a name like that?"

"I don't rightly know. They always called me Samantha at the orphanage, but Sister Elaine Catherine knew my mother and told me that was my birth name. This isn't about my name, it's about my shop. Many of you have seen me working hard over the past few months to bring you this wonderful place where you can buy books to read. I've also planned story-telling classes and if you'd like to learn to read, I will be setting up weekly classes for that, also. If you all follow along, I'll take you on a tour of my new book store."

"Can we get a cookie? I see cookies and lemonade over on that table." One of the men pointed to the snack table.

"Sir, when the tour is over, you can help yourself. Are you ready to tour my shop?" Her voice was firm. She wasn't going to put up with a beggar. If he wanted a cookie then the least he could do was take the tour. She almost giggled, but refrained and instead she began to stare at him with her serious blue eyes.

"I'm ready," he told her, his face downtrodden. Satisfied, she began the tour. "This is the children's section here," she explained to the crowd. There are over a hundred books right now to purchase. If you take notice, in the corner there are a pile of pillows stacked up high. There are ten pillows to be exact. Each week we will have a children's story time. There is a desk up front where you can sign up your child for a class for a small fee. There's more to come as well."

A few of the children began to run around the area, pulling books out of the display case. The excitement in their eyes always made Sam happy. She remembered how hard it was to learn to read until Sister Elaine Catherine taught her. Sam had so much to be grateful for. All she wanted was to pass the gift of reading on to the children of the world. Those who'd never pick up a book if it wasn't readily available. To Sam, if a child learned to read, she or he could go a long way. She believed that with every part of her mind and soul.

Some of the parents were getting upset about the children helping themselves to a book. She addressed the parents first. "If your child would like to sit on a pillow and look at a book while you tour the shop, it is permissible. I'd rather they get some enjoyment than be bored in my store."

Then, she turned to the children. "As long as your parents agree, I'll allow you to take a pillow and sit on the floor with one book at a time. When you are finished paging through, please put it back where you got it. If you don't follow instructions, then you won't be allowed to sit and look at a book."

Little heads nodded and promised to only take one at a time. Sam looked at the parents with raised brows. They all acknowledged Sam's instructions and followed her the rest of the way for a tour. Finally, they were at the cookie table. "Please, help yourself. Thank you for visiting today. If you have any questions, please ask. I'll be available until three this afternoon."

Sam crossed her fingers, stepped back and gave everyone room to browse. Her heart was pounding so fast, she took a few more steps back to make sure no one heard how wild her heart was beating even though she knew no one heard it but her. As she gazed around she wanted to shout out loud that she did it! All by herself, too.

That was not entirely true. She did have other people that did help. When she got to Cooper's Ridge, the reverend was so nice to her even though she was a tough-talking mouthy young woman at first. She had rode the train from Noel, Kansas with a couple that were moving here. She met them in Noel when everyone on the train had to ride out a horrible winter storm. They became friends and the couple helped Sam get here.

Sam owed Molly and her husband Harrison so much. When all of her traveling money was gone from having to stay the winter in Noel, they helped her get to Texas. Sam had paid them back as soon as she got a job at the stables. The last six months had been hard work, but Sam was proud of what she had accomplished, especially for an orphan girl.

A few women approached her carrying several books they wanted to buy. Sam smiled and rang them up, putting the books in colorful canvas bags she had made especially to carry purchased books. She had ordered them from a supplier in New York City who had printed **Sam's Book Shop** on the front of the bags. She realized they were more expensive than she wanted to pay, but knew advertising was the way to bring people to her store. The bags could be used for anything and how wonderful it would be to see women and men walking around Cooper's Ridge with her store brand on the front of their bags.

She also learned many residents left Cooper's Ridge on occasion to travel to other towns nearby. Her canvas bags would reach Wichita Falls, Mill Ridge and maybe even Dallas. Soon everyone would have heard about the woman owned book store here.

At least that was her intentions. Some people hated the idea that books would make them smart. Reading was not a priority for many, unfortunately. If it hadn't been for books, Sam wouldn't be where she was right now. Books were the reason she was here and she was going to help others see the truth of it all as well. She was going to work hard to change hard-nosed attitudes.

An hour and a half later the crowd began to die out. There were a few adults left in the store and one pretty young girl about six or seven years old. She wore a dark blue dress that was rather short. The hem only ended at her knees. Now Sam didn't know much about fashion, but she did know the girl was wearing an out of fashion dress that didn't fit her any longer. Which made her wonder who her parents were and where they were.

Standing back to observe, she watched as the other adults in the store finished shopping and checked out. Sam stayed busy and forgot about the girl until the book store was empty. When she looked up, the girl was still there, on a pillow on the floor paging through a book. Her pretty blonde hair was put up in two ponytails and she looked so serious as she tried to read the story.

Sam looked around again, wondering where her parents were. She had a sinking feeling the girl was used to spending time alone. Sam understood that more than anyone would ever know. Grabbing a pillow from the corner, she threw it on the floor near the young girl. "Would you mind if I sit down?"

The girl looked up, surprised to see Sam in front of her. "It's your store, isn't it? Of course you can sit wherever you want." She smiled at Sam, looking so serious. Yet, the lost look in her eyes was way too familiar to Sam.

Sam knelt down and sat on the pillow. "What are you reading?"

"I'm not really reading," she told Sam. "This is a favorite book of mine. It got ruined a few weeks ago when we moved out of our house."

"I'm sorry. Maybe your parents will buy you that one." Sam was never too shy about making a sale. It was what would keep her in business and she saw the opportunity. That is, until the girl kept talking. Once the child realized Sam was a nice adult, her words fell out of her mouth like a waterfall.

"My father won't. My father was mad because I forgot to pack it when we moved."

"I'm sorry. You can sit here and read it any time you'd like."

Her blonde pigtails shook when she nodded. "Thank you, ma'am."

"My name is Samantha but you can call me Sam."

"Sam is a boy's name."

Sam shook her head. "Not always. It's my name and I swear to it." She raised her right hand up in the air.

"My name is Chelsea Stevens. It's nice to meet you," she said, sounding so mature for her young age.

Sam gave her a smile. "It is a pleasure to meet you as well."

"We're on an adventure!" Chelsea had leaned in and spoke in a whispered voice.

Sam played along. "I love adventures. How is it you are on one right now?"

Chelsea motioned for Sam to get closer. "The girl in this book goes on an adventure so my father thought it would be good for us to go on one, too. That's why he was mad when I lost the book. Now we have to make up what happens to the girl since we never finished the book!"

"Isn't it wonderful that now you can read how it ends and finish your adventure?" Sam thought the whole idea of an adventure was quite strange. Something wasn't right here. Where was her father? Her mother also? She had been left alone here for over twenty minutes without anyone looking after her. Sam didn't like this one bit.

The bell above the door jangled. Sam turned to see who was entering her store. A tall man, dressed in a black jacket and slacks, a crisp white shirt and printed tie, along with a wide-brimmed cowboy hat walked in her store.

"Father!" Chelsea jumped up and ran to him, grabbing a hold of his pant leg and wrapping her arms around his leg. He bent down to her height, which didn't look easy but he managed to do so and gave his daughter a huge smile.

"I should've known you'd be here. I looked everywhere for you until the nice sheriff told me you might be at the book store opening since there were cookies and lemonade."

"I forgot about the cookies. Look what I found, Father!" She held the book up. When he saw the book, his face fell. He didn't look happy about the book at all.

She felt it was time to intervene. Samantha rose from the pillow. "Hello. I'm Sam, the owner of the store."

"Ma'am." He tipped the brim of his hat, then asked Chelsea to give him a minute while he spoke with her. Sam was curious now, more so than ever.

"Chelsea, you are welcome to have a cookie and some lemonade. Please help yourself," Sam told her. The girl didn't hesitate. She began to walk away from her father when he reached out and took the book from his daughter's hands.

Sam watched carefully as the young girl's face fell. He stared at the book, then his daughter. "Go on, get you a cookie."

As Chelsea hurried to the snack table, Samantha walked towards her father, holding out her hand. "Welcome to The Book Shop, Mr. Stevens."

Instead of taking her outstretched hand, he handed her the book. "My daughter doesn't need this," he told Sam, staring into her eyes.

Sam didn't understand why he was so rude. Most people were rude when they had something to hide or were scared. He didn't look like a man who got scared easily. What else was going on here? "Chelsea told me this is the same book you read to her every night."

"You mean used to read to her. She no longer has the book."

"There is one here to purchase," Sam offered.

The man shook his head. "We don't need it."

"Your daughter said she doesn't know how her adventure will end unless she reads the book."

The man stared at her. She knew the moment he recognized why she was pushing the issue. He was caught. "It's not any of your business."

She glared at him. Her hands went to her hips. "Maybe not, but she loves to read."

"She doesn't know how to read."

"It's obvious that you don't know either."

He blinked once then continued to stare, daring her to say it out loud.

Chapter 2

Sam didn't want to ruin the girl's perception of her father even though he'd been lying to her all along. So far, the conversation was spoken in low tones so Chelsea hadn't heard what they said to each other. When Sam looked over at the table, the girl was chomping on a cookie like she was starving.

Sam looked back at Mr. Stevens, noticing how handsome he was. Why she thought of that at a time like this was beyond her ability to reason. She never gave a man a second thought. Why him?

"She doesn't have a mother."

"What? That's your explanation as to why you are lying to her about the story?"

He shrugged. "It's a good enough one. Listen, you don't know the half of it."

Sam glanced at the clock. It was after three in the afternoon and she was officially closed. "I have time to listen. The store is closing."

He stared harder. "Seriously, it's none of your business. Chelsea lost her mother for the second time and I promised her an adventure hoping that will help. So I made up a few things in the book."

"You made the whole story up," Sam said. "The book is about a girl's brother getting lost and her searching for him, not an adventure."

He moved closer, a warning look on his face. "She doesn't know that and never will unless you tell her. My suggestion is to let it go. I don't need some fancy book lady trying to tell me how to raise my daughter!"

With those words, he called out to Chelsea. When she ran over, he took her hand and they left. Chelsea turned back and waved to her. "See you soon, Sam! I can't wait to come back again."

Sam watched as the two of them walked down the street. She turned the lock on the entrance door to make sure no one else came in. She was tired and ready to take a relaxing break with a cup of tea and one of her favorite books. She had worked so hard all week long to open the store and now that the first day was over, she wanted to reward herself with tea and a book.

She knew exactly which book she wanted to read. Picking up the book Chelsea had been holding, she turned the open sign to closed and pulled down the blind. She took her money box upstairs with her and opened the door to her neat apartment. Sam had only been here a few weeks, but she'd already furnished it with some nice pieces from Joseph Bodhi's woodworking shop.

Remembering the day she stopped in there, she had told Joseph she needed to furnish her empty apartment on a budget. He stared at her like she was crazy. Sam was afraid he'd ask her to leave. Then she realized he was assessing all of his furniture and then marched around his store finding her affordable pieces. His wife, Cordie, who had been a Pinkerton detective before she married Joseph, had given her some pictures to hang on her bare walls and flower vases and an oil lamp that was used for decoration purposes. "They'll do more good in your place than here," she told Sam. "Besides, I want to go shopping in Dallas so this is a good way to get ride of the old and bring in new."

Sam was appreciative of the gifts. She accepted the décor and turned her little apartment into her own comfortable place. It wasn't huge, only two rooms above the book store, but it was home until someday she'd be able to buy a house for herself. Sam wanted to find true love but for now she was satisfied with making the book store a success. It's all she thought about except when she thought about Chelsea's father.

He was quite handsome and his dark eyes made her heart go pitter-patter. Sam laughed to herself thinking about how he reminded her of this one hero in a dime novel she read about a few years ago. The hero was a gambler turned outlaw. He won every card game and took his earnings and gave it to the poor folks in this small western town. Then a gang of no-gooders came around and tried to scare the townsfolk. But first a rotten sheriff tried to make it look like it was the gambler who was doing bad things. So, the gambler turned outlaw had to prove his innocence. What a story that was.

Was Mr. Stevens like the gambler? Or was he a no-good father who took away his child's book because he lied to her about the story?

The reason he lied to his daughter about the story was because he couldn't read. No father should have an issue like that. If he didn't know how to read, then how was Chelsea ever going to learn? Perhaps the reason the child and then her father came into her shop was so she could teach them how.

Sam not only had a new book store to run, but she decided she needed to find out more about this family so she could help them. The girl just needed to know she could do anything this world throws at her, and somehow it seemed like her dad wasn't allowing that to happen. She was sure he had good reason, and she planned to get to the bottom of things.

Lord, as I speak and breathe, show me what it is you want me to do with little Chelsea and her father? I don't want to interfere but my

*gut instinct tells me they were sent here to Cooper's Ridge for a reason.
Just like I was. Thanks God. Amen.*

*****

Brent watched his adopted daughter sleep. She'd been restless ever
since they came back from the book store. The woman at the store
had been such a spitfire. Was it because she guessed his secret so
quickly? Or was it her beautiful spirit he noticed right away? It was
so refreshing to see someone interested in Chelsea. She had been
without her adopted mother for eleven months and Brent could
see how it had affected the child.

He loved Chelsea as if she were his own child. He left their
room, making sure she was tucked in tight, then sat out on the
porch at the boarding house to have a smoke. It was one habit he
found hard to break. Perhaps it was from his gambling days. He
didn't know. He lit the thin cigar and puffed on it once or twice
before letting it sit between his two fingers burning away.

The door opened and closed but he made no mind of it since
guests were coming and going all the time. He felt someone
standing near him, then the proprietor of the boarding house sat
on the chair beside his. "Is everything okay, Mr. Stevens? I peered
out the window and saw you staring for so long I became worried."

Brent smiled. "I'm fine, Miss Rachel." The older woman was so
sweet. She treated him and his daughter like they were family and
he appreciated all she was doing for them.

A hand was placed on his sleeve. "I know it's hard for you right
now. I want you to know that if you need anything, don't be afraid
to ask. For as long as you intend to stay, my boarding house is open
to you and Chelsea. She is such a pleasant child."

"She wants to learn to read," he blurted out.

"Well, why not? You and her are welcome to sit right out here on the porch or at my table when we aren't serving meals and teach her. It stays fairly quiet here."

Brent was uncomfortable admitting he wasn't able to help her. But, when he saw how much she yearned to be able to read the story, he gave it some thought and decided he'd try. Perhaps that book lady staring him down like she knew all his dirty secrets had made him realize he didn't want Chelsea growing up like he had.

Was he doing the same thing to her that his father did to him? He was so new at parenting, especially an orphan, but he wanted to do the best job he could.

So he had to start somewhere. "I can't read."

Another pat on the sleeve. "I'm sorry. That makes it more difficult. Wait a minute, I'll be right back." Miss Rachel hurried inside and came back out, her skirts swooshing as she sat back down, then read the paper out loud. "Sam's Book Shop's classes. Learn to read, every Monday and Thursday. Six in the evening. Classes cost twenty five cents per class. Sign up ahead of time in the book store."

He wondered what time it was. "Tomorrow is Sunday. The book store won't be open." He wanted to go knock on her door right now and sign up Chelsea so she could get started right away. It probably wasn't proper to do so.

"You can go to church and ask her. Sam will be there. Everyone goes to church unless there is a good reason not to."

He looked a little guilty since he hadn't gone to church last Sunday. Miss Rachel was quite aware and waited patiently for him to say something. Besides, if it was the only way to sign up Chelsea before Monday, then he'd go to church. "I'll be in church tomorrow. Chelsea will like that."

Miss Rachel stood. She had a bounce to her step as she went inside, telling him to make sure to close the door properly when he came in. Most of the guests were already settled in for the night. Brent stared at his cigar, then took another puff and put it out. He had a lot of bad habits to break.

One thing was for sure, he wanted Chelsea to grow up better than he had. If she was going to learn to read in Cooper's Ridge, he should probably see if there was a house to rent instead of staying at the boarding house.

*****

"Yes, Chelsea, we are going to church, now settle down some and eat your breakfast." He looked at Rachel, who was grinning. "I'm sorry, Miss Rachel, she is a bit overexcited that we are going to church."

"I'm so happy. I love to sing!"

At her outburst, Brent almost grinned but knew as a father, he needed to reprimand her not to speak out of turn even if he wanted to laugh instead. "Chelsea, manners."

She looked at Brent and blinked her eyes several times. Just like Sallie used to do. He shook himself. Sallie had been teaching her some bad habits. That was not how to get your own way, he thought. Brent wasn't going to say anything to her, he gave her a long stare and she put her head down and finished her breakfast in silence.

Miss Rachel finished serving the guests and sat at the head of the table. "I hope everyone enjoys breakfast. The church service will be long today and afterwards the reverend is having a dessert social, so save some room for sweet treats."

"Oh, I can't wait!" Chelsea burst out then placed a hand over her mouth. She gave her father an apologetic look.

He nodded, his throat constricted with memories of how they used to be as a family. Sallie, Chelsea and he made it a point to go out for breakfast every Sunday before church. Sallie liked to dress up and buy the most expensive food off the menu. When a man with more money came along she abandoned her husband and adopted daughter and ran off with him.

The anger he felt inside rose up. Brent had a heavy heart filled with unforgiveness. Especially since Sallie had wanted to adopt a child when the orphan train came to Dallas and he fell for it hook, line and sinker. Thinking he was changing his ways and becoming a family man, he jumped at the opportunity to marry Sallie since she said she wanted the same thing he did, a home and family.

He should've known when she wouldn't conceive any children of her own that something wasn't right. Instead, she saw the poster for the orphan train and told him they should adopt a child. He wanted his own child, but she insisted they take in someone elses. Since he was trying hard to change his ways and settle down, Brent agreed to the adoption.

Brent didn't regret ever adopting Chelsea since she became his anchor when Sallie left them both. He loved the child as his own and wanted to give her the world, but the burden of explaining why Sallie left had got to be too much day after day.

Chelsea would talk about Sallie every day. Then, she'd cry. It got to be too much for Brent. He sold the house they had recently bought and now was taking Chelsea on a grand adventure like in the book. Even though the book had a completely different story.

When Chelsea learned to read, was she going to hate him for lying to her?

"I'm ready to go to church now," her voice, so happy and delighted broke through his lost memories. Brent pushed away from the table and thanked Miss Rachel for a delicious breakfast. It was time to put the memories to rest and start thinking about a future.

Chapter 3

Sam was running late. Church was about to start in about twenty minutes and she still had another stall to muck. Even though she had opened her new book store, she wanted to keep earning money in case she had a few days where her income was lacking. Tom had agreed to keep her on at the livery on Sunday mornings as long as she was able to keep up with the two jobs.

Today she wasn't doing too well. She woke up a half hour late after spending the night thinking about little Chelsea and her father. Even though he left a bit angry, she was sure he'd come to his senses and allow the child to learn to read. Somehow, some way she'd have to make it happen for the child. And, for him. How do you raise a child and not be able to read?

So many folks did and she knew it was a common thread amongst the pioneers, putting their children to work in the fields and such, but if she was going to live here in Cooper's Ridge, then she'd make sure everyone surrounding her knew how to read.

Was she crazy? No, she was determined. Reading had saved her life and gave her dreams she wanted to pursue the moment she left the orphanage. Sam stopped to take a look at herself. Well, she was wearing men's britches and her vest and white shirt with cowboy boots that smelled to high heaven. She had her hair tied in one long braid as it swung over her shoulder.

She had to stop wasting time since she knew there would be no time to go home and change her clothing before church. As she took the shovel and cleaned the stall, she was more careful than ever not to step in the horse manure this time and drag it into the church. The last time she did that, everyone sat a few pews up from her. Which she didn't mind, no one bothered her the whole time during church. Well, maybe there were a few stares but she had thought at the time it was funny.

Now, she was a serious business woman and she needed all the support from the townsfolk she could get. She didn't want to anger any of them any more, not like she had when she first got here. Was she changing? Becoming more mature? Maybe so, although there was a side to her that didn't care either way. Sam wondered if that would ever change?

One thing she knew was that she had wanted to find her father and she had. Now, she was in a position to tell him who she was and yet every single time she saw him she found it impossible to tell him.

What if he rejected her? What if he would tell her that everything she knew about him was a lie and her mother was making it up? There were so many things standing in the way of just being honest with him.

Yet, she promised herself every single week after leaving church that she'd tell him. After all, God was on her side. She had prayed to him, asking her maker to help her find the right words. The strong connection while in church was always the one thing that had given her courage to confront him.

The moment she walked out of church, it was gone. It had been almost a year since she stepped foot in Cooper's Ridge and no one knew of her secret except for Sister Elaine Catherine and Molly Nelson, the new school teacher.

Sam met Molly in Noel, Kansas and helped her get to Cooper's Ridge. She knew about Sam's secret but promised not to say a word to anyone. Molly had been faithful all this time and never spoke of it again. There was one time she asked when Sam was going to confront him, but she wasn't ready. Molly had been her friend and was concerned, that's what she told Sam.

She finished up the stall, dumped the bucket filled with manure and headed back to the small wash basin to clean up. There was an area where Tom kept a pitcher and basin to clean up in. That would have to do for now. She had been careful not to get anything on her today and so far had been successful.

Sam heard the bells go off and knew it was the last call before church service started. She probably had about ten minutes to get there and slip into the back pew so no one would notice her even though every single person would turn in their seat to see her coming in late. Sometimes Sam wanted to stick her tongue out, then giggled when she realized that was not how a businesswoman should behave.

As she made her way to the church, the doors swung closed as someone else was getting there late also. She saw two figures go inside but was far enough away not to recognize who. She hurried up the steps, then pulled the door open to a full congregation.

As expected, every head turned to watch her stroll in the church in her men's britches and cowboy boots. The spur on the one heel made a noise on the wood floor and Sam grimaced as she realized she forgot to remove it. Now, she was even louder than before.

Pastor Murphy was at the front of the church and he stopped speaking as she walked in. At least he appeared amused and not upset. She gazed over the crowd in the last few rows and saw one open space in the very last pew. Right beside Mr. Stevens and his daughter, Chelsea.

There wasn't enough time to look for another place to sit, so she walked over and sat down as quickly and quietly as possible.

The townsfolk were still staring. Oh, how she wanted to stick out her tongue, then refrained. She clamped her jaw together and turned her head to look at Chelsea who was watching her with big, round eyes.

She didn't dare look at Chelsea's father. Maybe he wouldn't recognize her. All of a sudden, she realized the people were still staring at her because she didn't take her hat off. Sam reached up and pulled at it, placing the wide-brimmed hat in her lap. She kept staring straight ahead, making sure not to turn her head in fear of what she'd see on Mr. Steven's face.

As the pastor began to preach, she tried hard to listen but it was almost impossible now. Sam was going to get through this morning's sermon and than shoot out the door before anyone could stop her.

Of course, that wasn't going to happen. After prayer and a song, Pastor Murphy acknowledged the opening of Sam's Book Shop and everyone turned to her and began clapping. That was not how she wanted to start her day. She forced a smile and waved to the audience as it got quiet. Was she supposed to speak? Oh, not today!

The Sam these people knew would not apologize for coming to church in her britches so she wasn't about to start now even though she was turning a corner in her new life as a business woman.

She stood up and waved a hand in the air. "Thank you everyone! I don't deserve all of this attention, but I want to thank everyone for coming out on Saturday and supporting me in my new business. And please make sure to sign up your children for our reading group. I'd also like to encourage anyone who can't read to sign up for the adult reading class every Monday and Friday evening. You will be amazed at how easy it is to learn to read."

"I'm too old to learn to read," one of her favorite hecklers called out. She tipped her head and then shook a finger at him.

"Don't you spoil it for the young children, sir. I think you may benefit by coming to my classes."

"Yeah, old man, take some of that money you're hiding in your mattress and spend it on something worthwhile, like reading," one man from the congregation called out.

Which had everyone in the church laughing and making more comments. Sam gazed at Pastor Murphy. *I'm sorry,* she mouthed, never wanting to cause a spectacle.

He looked amused and waited patiently for everyone to settle down before raising a hand. "I think we should all help out our new business in town. I'll make a deal with you, Finley. If you go to every class of Miss Malone's, I'll reimburse you every penny you spend on learning how to read." He looked around the audience. "As a matter of fact, I'll reimburse up to five people. Now, if you don't want anyone to know you can't read, you just stop by Sam's, er, Miss Malone's shop and get put on the list." It didn't bypass her that he used her proper name. Everyone in town called her Sam but he was trying to be respectful. She was grateful for a chance to be shown some respect.

"This is quite generous of you, Pastor Murphy." On the other hand, she wanted to tell him that he was making a spectacle out of her right now but he was so nice she didn't have the heart. She still couldn't look at Mr. Stevens.

"Your speech at your grand opening made me realize you are a smart woman and we want people in town who care enough about this place and the people in it. Our school is coming along great and Molly is a fine teacher." Everyone clapped when he mentioned her, then settled down to let him finish. "To try to teach every single child and adult here to read is a huge task and Molly has her hands full with the children. I think this book store is one of the best things to come to Cooper's Ridge."

"If you say so, Pastor!" One of the hecklers had to throw in the last line. Some of the others laughed, but mostly everyone told him to hush his mouth. Sam was so fortunate to not only have a chance to help others learn to read but now she had a chance to make sure Chelsea was allowed to. She had to confront Mr. Stevens.

"Church is officially over for now. I've got a surprise for all of you," he told his congregation.

"It's no surprise, Pastor Murphy. We saw the desserts being loaded up earlier. Everyone knows we're having a dessert social!"

Pastor Murphy shook his head. "I can't keep anything from you, can I?" he teased and began shaking hands.

Sam finally turned to speak with Mr. Stevens. "Excuse me, sir. Do you have a moment?"

He nodded, and then his jaw moved up and down then clamped shut.

She stared, waiting for him to begin speaking. Chelsea jumped in first. "My father wants to sign me up for reading class. He told me on the way here this morning."

She was so surprised and delighted as well. Sam's eyes lit up and she knew they were shining brightly. She took Chelsea's outstretched hand and held it for a moment. "I'm so happy. Will I see you tomorrow?"

She nodded. "My father told me I can take all the classes I want to so I can learn to read."

"That's wonderful, Chelsea. I'll see you tomorrow evening at six." She knew they were passing through on their adventure and all, but a girl like Chelsea needed school. She turned to Mr. Stevens before leaving the church. "I have four more slots to fill courtesy of Pastor Murphy. Can I expect to see you taking on one of them."

He glared at her like nobody's business. Those dark eyes hardened before her very eyes and she knew then he was embarrassed to let his daughter know that he couldn't read. Sooner of later she'd find out. But that was up to him to tell her. Come to find out she didn't have to say a word. Chelsea turned to her father.

"Father, you can come too! Pastor Murphy said he'd do something if five people went. I think you probably need to learn to read too. Sometimes I don't think you're saying the right words."

There it was! Sam saw the regret in his eyes and the sadness that he let his daughter down. Even if she wasn't entirely aware of it. Sam watched as he swallowed hard and nodded. "I'll be there," he told them both. "Let's go, Chelsea. There's a dessert social starting without us."

Sam was left standing in the church as everyone emptied out the pews row by row. She won and yet she felt absolutely empty inside. The fact she saw Mr. Stevens at his most vulnerable had him disliking her.

She saw it on his face. His eyes were cold and his demeanor abrupt. This was not going to be easy. She smiled to herself. It would be a challenge she was willing to take.

As she left, Pastor Murphy stopped her. "Sam! There might be more than five townsfolk coming to your class. Will you have room for more?"

Sam thought about it. "I prefer to keep the classes small, but if more people want to learn to read, Pastor Murphy, I'll open up more classes."

He looked happy to hear that. "I didn't realize so many folks in town can't read. You're going to be busy for a long time. Listen,

Sam, no matter how many people sign up, you tell them they'll be reimbursed for their class if they finish. I don't want anyone to be refused."

She didn't know what to say. Pastor Murphy was so kind from the start, but now he was her hero. "Thank you. I'll do my best to make this town proud."

"I'm sure you will. Remember what I said. No one gets turned away."

"Yes, sir. I better go spend the day preparing for tomorrow's class."

"Not until you have some dessert first, Sam!"

She waved and decided it wouldn't hurt to spend a few minutes at the social. Since it was such a lovely summer day, the dessert social was held outside in the church yard. Tables were set up to accommodate the food. Many folks sat down on the grass with their families and enjoyed the day.

Sam wanted the delightful cherry cobbler she spotted. "I don't know who made that, but I have to try it," she told Catherine, Pastor Murphy's wife, who was behind the table handing out servings.

"There is a new bakery in town and Charlie Baxter who owns the restaurant is not happy as he thinks he'll lose customers. It won't hurt him one bit," she told Sam.

"This is delicious," she told the pastor's wife, who was helping to serve others as well. She turned to Sam.

"Did anyone ever tell you how your eyes sparkle when you look happy?"

"No one ever told me that," she mumbled since her mouth was full of the delectable pie.

"I only noticed it since my husband's eyes sparkle like that. Most of the time he's so busy with his work and ministry that his focus is so intense on what he is doing. I worry he misses the small things in life sometimes but then he gets so happy and his eyes sparkle like yours do and that's all I need to know so I don't worry about him. Whew! That was a mouthful."

Sam giggled in between bites of her pie. Whoever the new baker in town was, he knew how to bake. "I'm going to have to visit this bakery at some point," she told Catherine.

"Please do. I'll go with you when you're available. We can get a cup of coffee and something sweet."

"I'd love to." She finished her dessert and looked around to find the pan where the dirty dishes would be placed.

"I'll take that for you," Catherine told her, stretching her arms across the table. "Why don't we plan to visit the bakery in the next week or two?"

"Stop by the book store anytime, Catherine. Unless it is Monday or Thursday. Those days I have class."

"It's a deal." Catherine waved as Sam left the social. Now that she knew she wouldn't be standing around her store waiting on people to show up for her class, she had to put a plan in place. With five students, she'd have to make room. The food table for her grand opening had been placed near the rear of the store. She had placed stacks of books on it, but they could be removed. They'd use the area for a classroom since it was quiet near the rear of the store.

As she thought about what to teach on the first day, she wasn't paying attention to where she was going and ran into Mr. Stevens. He caught her elbow.

"Are you all right? I'm very sorry," he told her.

She shook herself. "I'm afraid it was my fault. I had my head in the clouds, so to speak," she answered.

He grinned. "I guess we both did."

That made her laugh. "Well, then. I'd say we are even. See you tomorrow evening for class."

"Who will I see, Sam the stable girl dressed in britches or Samantha the book lady?"

Sam's eyes lit up with laughter. "One never knows. I guess you'll have to show up to find out!" With those words, she turned and walked down the street, laughing to herself. Indeed!

Chapter 4

Sam looked around with approval. She had lugged the large rectangular table over towards the back wall of the store and placed five chairs around it. Then, she placed a pencil, sheets of paper and a book at each spot. Since it was later in the day when the classes would start, she already planned to have lanterns close by.

Hopefully, there was no need to use a lantern. At least not in the middle of the summer, but on some days when it got stormy outside later in the afternoon, a lamp would cast enough light in the store.

Since she had opened at nine in the morning, folks had wandered into her store. There was foot traffic mostly in the morning, then it died off around the noon hour. Later in the afternoon, things got busy again. She was glad to see so many townsfolk interested in books.

Knowing it wasn't going to make her rich, Sam didn't care about that. She had what she worked hard for; a book store that was of her own making. Coming from an orphanage and travelling halfway across the country made all the hard work worth everything.

No one was ever going to take this away. She'd work more hours at the livery if things got slow. She hoped her ideas for classes where she'd be able to teach the townsfolk something they were interested in would go over well. There was a ton of things she could teach in her book store.

Whatever she had to do to keep her doors open, Sam had every intention of doing. Right now, she was about to teach a class of adults and one child how to read.

There was a large grandfather clock in the corner of the store that had been here when she moved in. As time tumbled forward, every click of the second hand echoed louder and louder until a movement at the front door caused her to stop staring at the face of the clock.

Mr Finley opened the door, cautiously looking in, then took a step inside. She waited until he was inside before speaking. "Good evening, Mr. Finley. I'm so happy you are here."

He seemed surprised and lifted a hand in the air. "I'm only here because Pastor Murphy made a spectacle of me in church. I sure don't want people saying I was too chicken to learn to read."

She smiled. "No one would think that of you, I'm sure."

He glared at her as specks of grey in his dark hair covered his forehead. He was in need of a good cut, she thought, but didn't mention that to him since it was just her opinion. Maybe he liked his hair in his eyes. He'd see much better, she did know that much. "There's plenty of folks who'd make fun of me. They always do."

"We're going to change that, Mr. Finley."

"Name's Finley. Ain't no mister."

She was curious. "Do you have a last name, Finley?"

He shook his head, then shrugged. "No idea. I've always been called Finley."

She didn't know how to respond to that. "Why don't you look around the bookshelves and pick out the first book that catches your attention. I'd like you to take it with you back to the table where we'll be learning." She pointed to her table set up in the rear of the store.

He nodded and started to walk around the store as if it were a challenge. Satisfied he was taking an interest even if he acted as if he wasn't, Sam went to the door when a young mother and her young baby came through. "Hello, are you here for the class?"

She nodded, and asked if the baby would be a problem. When Sam assured her the baby was welcome, she went to the children's section and took four pillows and laid them out side by side. The young mother placed the child on the pillows and covered her with a small blanket she brought along. "There you go, sweet Isabell. I hope you sleep well so I can learn." The mother stood and thanked Sam. "I have two dollars to pay for eight classes. You said twenty-five cents a class, right?"

"Yes, and if you'd like to tell me your name, I'll mark that you are paid."

It's Mary Trenton. My husband is James Trenton. We just came here last week and plan to buy a house from Pastor Murphy. He told me that I can learn to read and it would help me raise my daughter better."

"Pastor Murphy is right. He'll also reimburse you the two dollars when you finish the classes."

"That's wonderful. My husband doesn't make much but we get by. Our rent is pretty cheap. This is a nice town."

Sam hadn't seen Mary or her husband James before. She had been so busy getting ready for her grand opening, she probably never saw them come to town. They did have folks who came for a few days and left soon after when they realized the rules the pastor insisted people live by were too strict for them.

"Rent? Do you mind telling me who you rent from? I'm thinking about staying for a while."

The young woman nodded and smiled. "Pastor Murphy rented out a house to us. They're at the end of the street, across from his church."

Sam turned to find Mr. Stevens and Chelsea right behind her. She never heard the door open or the jingle of the bell above since she had been so intent on making sure the baby had a soft bed to lie on. "Good evening, Mr. Stevens. Hello, Chelsea."

"Hello. I'm ready to learn to read," the young girl told Sam.

"While I have the three of you here, let me explain what we are doing. I'd like each one of you to walk around the store and the first book that catches your eye, pick it up and take it with you to the table in the rear of the store. Find a seat and we'll start as soon as everyone gets here."

"Are you expecting a lot more?" Mary asked.

"No. I believe five is the limit. I like to keep my classes small. If anyone else shows up, we'll have them start on another evening."

"If you have day classes, I'd rather move to days," she told Sam. "It's the baby and all and then James gets home from working so hard and I have to rush to get here on time."

Sam nodded. "I'll take note of that and keep you first on the list for daytime classes."

"Thank you, Sam. You are so kind."

She turned to welcome four men who wanted to sign up for classes. "Gentlemen, I have room for one more for this evenings class. Which one of you would like to join today's class?"

After rearranging the schedule, Mary decided to come back tomorrow during Sam's day class she had just added. Two of the men stayed while the others promised to return in the morning. Satisfied, she asked everyone to take a seat so they could begin.

Sam was in full force as she explained why she had them each choose a book. "I want you to keep the book at all times. Bring it to class. Take it home with you but do not lose it. By the time we are finished here, you will be able to read that book you picked out. Maybe we'll have each person read to the class."

The two men who came in last, Larry and Jim Miller were twin brothers who looked alike. It was easy to tell them apart since Larry was thin and Jim wasn't.

Larry piped up. "I guess I should've picked a skinnier book."

Jim shook his head. "I told you to go to the children's books, you idiot."

Sam intervened. "Now, fellows. No name calling in my class."

Jim apologized and they moved on. Sam had everyone's full attention for almost a full hour. She noticed when Chelsea got a bit antsy, her foot kept kicking the table leg, making a thumping sound. Several times her father reprimanded her but she fell right back into thumping her foot without even realizing it. "I think we'll wrap it up for this evening. Thank you all for coming and I'll see you Thursday. Are there any questions before you leave?"

She glanced at everyone at the table. Finley had an elbow on the table with his chin in his hand and let out a huge snore.

"Finley, wake up!" Jim and Larry both shouted to him at the same time.

Chelsea started to laugh and her father followed suit. Sam didn't help by starting to giggle. When Finley woke up, he grumbled before asking if the class was over yet.

Sam sighed. "Finley, would you rather have morning classes so you don't fall asleep?"

He shook his head and got up from the chair. "Nope. I like this just fine."

Sam worried that he wasn't going to be a good student. "Okay, Finley, but if you fall asleep during class, I'll have to move you to days. We can't have all that snoring disturbing the rest of the students."

He grumbled about being treated unfairly but Sam ignored him and said goodbye to Larry and Jim as they headed out. Finley called out for them to wait up and followed them out the door.

Mr. Stevens and Chelsea were taking their time to leave. She noticed how Chelsea tucked her book under her arm. "I can't wait until Thursday," she told Sam. "Goodbye."

"Hold on a second, Chelsea." Mr. Stevens turned to Sam. "I hope I'm not being over enthusiastic, but it looks like you still have two more openings tomorrow. Would you mind if Chelsea and I come to the morning class as well? I'd really like for us to get all the teaching we can until we have to leave on our adventure."

Sam wasn't sure she wanted to have him here two days in a row. He did something to her even though teaching his daughter was in the child's best interest. Even Mr. Stevens deserved to know how to read. Except he was so disturbing to look at, in a good way. It was her heart that was beating so fast she could barely think during class.

"Just how long do you plan to be in town before you go off to finish this adventure of yours?"

"Father said we're going to stay here for a while. I'm glad. I like it here." She twirled around and that's when Sam noticed how short the hem of her skirt was. When she stared even harder at the girl, she saw the threads were so snug at her shoulders. Chelsea needed to be wearing clothes that fit her. What she wore was way too tight.

"Is there something wrong?" Mr. Stevens asked, frowning. He was so aware of everything Sam did and said. How was she supposed to deal with him?

"Perhaps we can talk another time. I'd be happy to add you to the morning class. Be here at ten sharp."

Sam watched the two of them leave. She smiled when Chelsea took her father's hand and began to skip, pulling him forward as he almost ran to keep up. They were laughing and she joined in from inside the store window, her voice echoing at the same time the clock struck eight.

Sam locked the door and carried the oil lamp upstairs with her. It had been a long day, but she was so satisfied with the way things went. She not only had a store that was selling quite a few books but a class that was paying off. She sighed. Hopefully, she'd be able to keep up with the demand.

It didn't matter. Sam would persevere no matter what. In that way, she was more like her father. A little voice inside asked her when she was going to tell him who she was.

Not yet. She wasn't quite ready.

Chapter 5

Brent had to carry Chelsea up the stairs and tuck her into bed. She was so exhausted from being up so late. "Sweet dreams, Sunshine," he told her.

"I love you, Father," she mumbled. It was barely a whisper but he heard her little voice. Taking the glasses from her face, he carefully laid them on the small table beside the bed and kissed her forehead.

"I love you, Chelsea."

Brent watched her sleep for a few more minutes, then went back downstairs and out the door of the boarding house for a smoke. He really didn't need it tonight, but out of habit, he lit up and let it burn between his fingers once again.

The boarding house was quiet. He was glad to be here and have breakfast made for them each morning and an evening meal if they wanted one, but Brent was feeling unsettled. He wanted this adventure he promised his daughter to end and settle down.

Except he wasn't sure where to settle. Deep in his thoughts, he caught the sheriff strolling across the street. "Brent. You still up?"

"It's a quiet night," he told the sheriff. "What about you? What are you doing up so late?"

"I'm doing my job. My deputy had an emergency this evening so I had to work later. Turns out he's having a lot of emergencies several times a week. May have to find me a new deputy soon." The sheriff looked frustrated. "It's hard to find a good man for the job."

"Sounds like you have something more important to go home to," Brent mentioned.

"I do. A wife and a sweet adopted daughter Janey. I vowed to slow down and hired a deputy, but he's not turning out to be too reliable."

"Sorry to hear that, Sheriff."

The sheriff stared at Brent for a slight moment. "What brings you to Cooper's Ridge?"

He knew this was coming. Brent usually dressed like a gambling man since he was one for so long. Some habits were hard to break. "Passing through."

The sheriff nodded. "How long do you plan to stay?"

"I'm not sure. My daughter Chelsea thinks we're going on a new adventure."

"Are you?"

"It started out that way until I could find us a new place to live. She doesn't know it yet."

The sheriff pushed his hands deep in his pockets, balancing himself on the heels of his boots. He leaned back and perused Brent. "Any reason you need a new place to live?"

Brent was tired. He was trying to learn how to read and it had been a long day. "My wife ran off with a rich man, Sheriff, if that's what you want to know. We lived in Dallas until I couldn't stand seeing Chelsea so sad. She waited by the window every night for Sallie to come home until I finally had to tell her that her mother was not coming back."

"I'm sorry."

"So am I. It isn't easy raising a child alone. Sallie and I met in Dodge City. She was a dancer and I was a gambler. She got caught trying to steal and I stuck up for her. The rest is history."

"I think I know where this is going. You don't have to explain, Brent."

"You know my name?"

"I know everyone's name who comes to my town," he told Brent.

"I guess you do. I was a bounty hunter for a few months before I became a gambler. Gambling was much easier but it was a life I no longer wanted. I tried to settle down and thought I loved Sallie. She didn't want any kids though. That should've been my sign but I insisted."

"Sounds like you're better off without her."

"Yeah, we are. When I kept at her about settling down and starting a family, she suggested we get a kid from the orphan train. She didn't want a baby even though I did."

"Sounds like you were the one to always be compromising."

"I guess you're right. We got Chelsea a year and a half ago. She spent five months with the child then fell for some gambler and took off one night. Left me a dang note that she wasn't ever coming back."

"You get a divorce?"

Brent nodded. "Sure did."

"Probably for the best."

"Yeah." Brent ran a hand through his hair. "I have full custody of Chelsea, too. Not that Sallie cares. She left the girl high and dry."

"I better get home." The sheriff turned back. "Cooper's Ridge is a good place to start over. Everyone here is either a redeemed outlaw or wanting a second chance."

"I might stay awhile. I don't know. Right now, Chelsea is learning to read. So am I," he admitted.

The sheriff nodded. "Best of luck to you."

"Thanks, Sheriff."

The sheriff tipped the brim of his hat again. "If you're planning to stay awhile, you may want to free up your room at the boarding house and rent a house from Pastor Murphy. It'll be a lot cheaper."

"Maybe I will, although money isn't an issue. I saved enough from my gambling days right before I quit."

"Sounds like you were planning ahead, son. If you need a job, come see me. I may have a deputy position open before the week is up."

The conversation with the sheriff was a lot to take in. Brent sat back and relit his cigar. Drawing in on the end, he

blew smoke back out and sighed. He had to think more. Settling down here might be the right thing to do.

Would he be able to raise Chelsea in a town like this? There was a school, a church and everything for a child to grow up in. There were women here he could get to know. Was it possible to start over here?

He closed his eyes, drawing in the sweet smell from the cigar. The book lady's sweet smile was all he thought about before he went inside to get some rest. Brent had a class to go to in the morning.

He wanted to be at his best to learn to read. Or, perhaps he just wanted to see her. The book lady.

*****

Sam turned the sign from closed to open and unlocked the door. It was a lovely day so she stepped outside for a few minutes watching the world go by. Wagons rolled down the street, either coming or going, she wasn't sure which.

A woman and her two children walked by causing Sam to smile. "Good morning. I see you are using the book bag from my shop."

The woman nodded. "It comes in so handy. We're going to Mill Ridge to visit my aunt. I can't wait to tell her about your store."

Her words made Sam giddy. She was hoping the advertisement on the bags would make a difference. Crossing her fingers behind her back, she wished them a safe trip and hurried back inside.

She put out fresh paper and sharpened the pencils on the rectangular table where she planned to teach from. She'd have to keep the book store opened, but it was mid-week and she expected the customers would stagger in throughout the day.

If it became a problem, she'd have to close from ten to eleven to teach the class. Maybe having it while her store was open would convince others who needed some help to sign up.

Chelsea and Mr. Stevens were the first to show up. Chelsea carried her book under her arm and hugged Sam's skirt when she came through the doors. It was a nice feeling. She thought Chelsea was so well mannered.

Mary and baby Isabell came next. The baby was wide awake so Sam took her for a few minutes while Mary got settled. When she turned, Mr. Stevens was standing there, looking dumbfounded and staring at the baby. He looked up to see Sam watching him before shaking himself like a dog who just wet his fur.

"I see Pastor Murphy outside. Excuse me for a minute, please. Do you mind? I need to see him about an important matter."

"Of course," she told him, bewildered. That was the strangest reaction she had ever seen. Mr. Stevens had stared at her as if she was the most important person in the world just then. Sam was a bit overwhelmed by it all. Why had he looked at her that way?

She gave the baby back to Mary and welcomed the other men who hadn't stayed last night. Joe and Marvin Healey were also brothers who wanted to learn to read. They were quiet and withdrawn, which was unusual. Usually one brother was rowdy and the other quiet.

She instructed them both to find a book and sit down at the table. "We'll be starting as soon as Mr. Stevens returns." Sam stretched her neck to see him still speaking with Pastor Murphy. Sam waved to the pastor and pointed to her clock on the wall, then to Mr. Stevens. She wasn't sure if the pastor realized she was on a time schedule, but he nodded and cut the conversation short, sending Chelsea's father back in the book store.

"Thank you for returning, Mr. Stevens. Please take your seat so we may begin."

"I have some news for Chelsea. We're going to be staying here in Cooper's Ridge for a while. I'll be able to enroll her in school."

"That's wonderful news," Sam told him. "Go tell her right now. As a matter of fact, go enroll her in school."

"I'd rather surprise her after the class."

"You still want to continue the classes?"

"Chelsea will be in school to learn to read, but yes, I want to continue. It's important for her to know that I'm taking this seriously."

"I'm very proud of you, Mr. Stevens. Now I can be hard on you and Chelsea won't see that," she teased.

He grinned. "It looks like you'll have to put up with me for some time. I'm a slow learner."

She shrugged. "Not the way I teach. You'll learn quick or -"

He leaned closer. "Or what?"

Sam's eyes grew wider. "I don't rightly know," she admitted. "Now, please have a seat so we can carry on. It's only an hour long class."

Mr. Stevens did as she asked, and she began by holding letters in the air and having each person repeat the sound she made. This went on for most of the hour allotted to them. When they were done, the two brothers, Marvin and Joe Healy looked smitten. "I can't wait until Thursday's class," Marvin told her. He took her hand and bowed low over it. "Miss Sam, you are the best teacher in the world."

"Oh dear! It's Miss Malone, Marvin. I think you should address me as such during class. Afterwards, you can call me Sam like you always do."

"Class is over, so I'll call you Sam."

She walked the two men to the door and closed it roughly the moment they left.

"I believe you have admirers, Sam." Mary gathered her baby, who had fallen asleep on the pillows that were put out for her earlier.

Chelsea jumped up and down. "What are admirers? Can I have one?"

Her father shook his head. "No, Chelsea. You are too young. That is someone who is fond of another person."

"I'm fond of you, Father. Am I an admirer?"

Mr. Stevens looked flustered. Sam stepped in. "I believe you have some good news for Chelsea. Why don't you tell her now?"

Mr. Stevens nodded, glad to change the subject by the look of relief on his face. "Come here, Sunshine." Chelsea wandered over to her father, still jumping up and down some. "I've spoken to Pastor Murphy this morning and he has a house for rent."

"That's nice. What's for rent mean?"

"It means that you and I can stay here in Cooper's Ridge for a while and you get to go to a real school."

"I do!" When her father nodded, Chelsea jumped up and down so much both Mr. Stevens and Sam were laughing so loud it sounded like there were ten people in the store.

"We'll have our own house and I can make friends and then I can learn to read and can I get a puppy?"

"A house and school are enough for now," he told her.

Her face fell and she looked sad. "What about our adventure, Father? I know you wanted to go on it really bad and I did too but I like it here."

Sam wanted to pull Chelsea into her arms and give her a giant hug. Instead, she watched her father do it. "Oh, Sunshine. I don't know how long we'll stay. Maybe we'll be here forever. Let's take it slow and see how we like Cooper's Ridge."

"I love it here already and can't wait until tomorrow to go to school. Can I go to school tomorrow?"

"Yes. We should go see Miss Molly at the schoolhouse and get you registered. She'll be happy to have you, I'm sure."

Sam wanted to help and she wasn't sure how to go about suggesting the child needed new clothes. She didn't want to offend Mr. Stevens so she tried to be as delicate as possible. "I have an idea! Since I don't have any classes this evening and my shop closes at three, I'd love to take Chelsea and get her a few new outfits for school, that is, if you don't mind, Mr. Stevens?"

He looked so relieved she was glad to have spoken up. "I would love your help," was all he said.

"Good. Then let's plan on meeting here at three sharp. I believe I have a customer. Good day." Sam went about taking care of a customer while the two left the store. Mr. Stevens looked back twice before he actually closed the door.

Sam wasn't sure what this afternoon would bring but she wanted to find out.

Chapter 6

At ten minutes until three, Sam went to the front of the store to see if the two were on their way. She was getting so excited to take Chelsea shopping. God knew the girl needed new clothes. Besides, kids were so cruel at times. Sam knew better than most kids that her short dress would be made fun of at some point.

She never forgot her days at the orphanage and never would. Hopefully what she learned could be carried over and taught to Chelsea. Sam frowned. What was she thinking? The Stevens' may not be around for more than six months. Mr. Stevens never said he was staying forever.

All Sam knew was this had become a real home to her. She didn't want to ever leave now that she found a place here. Why she thought the two of them would be here forever astounded her. She had to stop thinking like this. As if she had a future with them.

At approximately two fifty-nine Chelsea ran up to the door and turned to wait for her father. He hurried behind her then picked her up and threw her onto his shoulders. Chelsea began giggling so hard Sam joined in. She swung open the door and laughed. "Let me lock up and we'll be on our way."

She was surprised Mr. Stevens wanted to come along. "I can bring her to the boarding house when we are through if you'd like, Mr. Stevens. I don't mind doing so."

He shook his head. "I can't leave you to go shopping with this wild one. You'll need me to keep her in check."

Chelsea laughed harder and pulled on her father's ears. He yelped and pretended like he was going to let her fall from his shoulders.

Sam knew he was joking but she yelled out loud. "Oh my goodness!"

The three of them laughed even harder as they walked down the street. He was laughing so hard, he had to slide Chelsea off his shoulders and stop for a minute. He looked right at Sam. "This is one of the best days of my life."

Sam's heart went out to him. He was a man who had his heart broken by his wife and was trying to figure out how to raise a young girl on his own, even pretending to be able to read her a story without the ability to read. She looked at him with a new respect. He was everything a husband and father should be. His wife had been a fool. Sam was going to teach him to read like nobody's business.

"Here we are. I saw the sign on the window the other day. It's the perfect place for a new school dress."

Chelsea took Sam's hand as they went inside. She had one hand in Sam's and the other in her fathers. It was almost as if they were a family. "Can I get a pair of britches like you wear?"

Sam didn't know how to react or what to say. Luckily, her father stepped in this time, saving her from saying anything at all.

"I don't believe britches are allowed in school. Girls have to wear dresses and boys wear britches. That's the rule." He looked over Chelsea's head and winked at Sam. She sighed.

"That's a dumb rule. I'm going to tell my new teacher about Sam's britches. Maybe she'll change the rules."

"You have to listen to your teacher," Mr. Stevens warned her.

Sam kept her mouth closed. The only reason she started out wearing men's clothes was to travel by herself. Perhaps it was time to explain why she wore them to the girl. It would be easier on Chelsea if she understood. She made it a point to have that conversation with her at some point today. Meanwhile, there were rows of clothes in ladies and children's sizes in the store she wanted to see.

Chelsea ran over to one long row of colorful dresses with sharp patterns and began to dive in, looking at each dress.

Sam looked at her father. "Thank you for your help today, Mr. Stevens. She asks a lot of questions."

He smiled at her. It was so genuine that she felt a warmth rise from her inside. Their eyes met briefly but she looked away, pretending to be watching Chelsea. "I'd like it if you'd call me Brent. That's my name."

"Thank you. I think we are two people concerned about one small young lady which makes us friends, so Brent it is."

"I like the way you say my name," he told her. His voice was soft, as if he was suggesting there was more between them than a friendship. She wanted to run out of the store as fast as her legs would take her but stood as still as a bird on the edge of a rocky ledge with loose stones.

She mustered up the nerve to speak. "Then perhaps I should continue to call you Mr. Stevens. Since I'm considered your teacher that you are paying a fee to learn to read, and you are considered my student, it would be in our best interest to keep it teacher and student, nothing more."

He grinned. "I wasn't suggesting anything more."

Sam glared at him. "Yes, you did. You whispered in my ear how you like the way I say your name. To me, that is being suggestive."

He laughed. "Sam, I think you are making too much of that. I was just saying how I like the way my name rolls off your tongue."

She shook her head. "You said no such thing about a tongue." She closed her mouth. Each time she came back with something else he confused her even more.

"I'm sorry. You're right, I'm teasing you. I meant well but you are so much fun to have fun with."

"I'm so much fun to have fun with?" His words stopped her. She was about to lash out when she realized that was a compliment.

"Yes, but I think we should pay attention to Chelsea. She has three dresses over her head at the moment."

"Oh!" Sam made her way to Chelsea and helped her get two of the dresses off. "One at a time, darling child. Let's see how this one looks on you first."

The length was perfect. "You look beautiful," she whispered to Chelsea. The child smiled and lifted her head a notch.

By the time she had tried all three dresses on, Sam looked at Brent, who seemed visibly upset. He stood back a bit then left. A few minutes later, he came back. "I left money at the counter for the dresses. Please get her shoes and anything else she needs. I'll be outside."

"Brent? Is something wrong?"

He shook his head and left the store, the bells notifying Sam when he walked out. She was clearly confused at his reaction. *What happened?*

"Sam, can I get one of these too?" Sam tried to pay attention to Chelsea as she asked for ribbon for her hair that she couldn't say no to. When they were done, they took the goods to the front of the store and waited until the owner came out of the back.

Several minutes later, the two left the shop with their hands full. Chelsea was so delighted she had beautiful dresses to wear for school. Sam looked around to see where Brent was at and found him across the street speaking with the sheriff. She waved until he saw them and came back across.

"Did you find everything, Chelsea?"

"I did, Father. Thank you! I can't wait until tomorrow. I'm so excited."

He took the items from her arms then turned to Sam. "We're going to go to our new house. Would you like to come along?"

She really shouldn't. "Of course."

"Can we go to the café for supper?"

"Yes, Sunshine. Only if Sam comes along."

"I really shouldn't."

"Aren't you hungry? We worked hard to get me new dresses," Chelsea told her in such an innocent tone that there was no way Sam would refuse the child.

"I suppose I can come along this time."

"Goodie!"

"Manners, Sunshine."

Chelsea blushed and actually apologized to Sam. "I'm sorry, Sam. It's just that I'm so happy you're here."

She smiled at the child. "I'm happy to be here. Now, we better get these pretty dresses to your new house."

They walked towards the church, then crossed the street where four houses were sitting side by side. They were all identical in nature with a small front porch and no business attached. Brent went through the small white gate and up the steps first to unlock the door. "Here we are," he told them.

When they went in, Sam was surprised at how roomy the sitting area was. There was already a settee and several upholstered chairs sitting side by side. The kitchen was roomy with a cook stove and a round table that seated four. A bench and two chairs surrounded the table. There was also a door that led to the back of the house. "It looks like you'll have a nice yard to play in," Sam told Chelsea.

"Can I go look?" she asked, jumping up and down again, the two ponytails jumping all over.

"Yes. Come right back in though."

When Chelsea went through the door, Brent turned to her. "Sam, I'm sorry I left you alone in the store to deal with my child. I had to leave."

She wanted to understand what happened. "Why did you?"

He shook his head. "When I saw how beautiful she looked in her new school dress, I realized how I failed her."

"What? I don't understand."

"I didn't even realize her dresses were too short. No one said a word to me. For all these months I've been putting clothes on my child that were too tight. She looks so much better now with the proper clothing. I was so ashamed of myself."

Sam was relieved, yet his words were upsetting. "Don't kick yourself in the foot about it, Brent. How were you to know? This is clearly Sallie's fault for running off and leaving you to deal with a child all of a sudden."

"I was too embarrassed to ask anyone for help." His simple statement floored her. Yes, he was right. There were many people in Dallas that would've helped him. Even if he'd have walked into a shop and asked the proprietress what was proper, he could've save himself embarrassment. "By not asking, I caused more harm than good with Chelsea."

Sam placed a hand on her hip and shook a finger at him. "That will be enough feeling sorry for yourself, Brent. You did what not a lot of men will not do. Do you realize that you had a choice to keep her or give her back to the orphanage?"

"Well, yes, but -"

"You didn't send her back. You chose to keep her and raise her as your own. Do you know how many children would die to be in her place?"

"How would you know?"

"I was raised in an orphanage, too. I'm one of those children that would've given my right arm to have a home. I don't ever want to hear how you ruined the child because of a silly mistake with her dresses. You, sir, have no excuses from my point of view."

He stared at her for almost a minute. Sam stood there with her hand on her hip and her face was flushed. She watched as his face went from guilty to angry to joyous. He came forward like a man on a mission.

Sam took a step back. Whoa! What was he doing? He pulled her into his arms and placed a kiss on her mouth she never had time to see this coming. They shared the most intimate of kisses before he pulled back, lifted his face into the sky and roared with laughter. "You, Sam are one of the most delightful women I've ever met."

She had nothing to say. Any chances of speaking at the moment were non-existent. He had kissed her to silence!

"Father! Did you just kiss Sam?"

Her father turned to her. "Yes, I did and if you tell a soul we won't be able to go to the eatery tonight together."

Sam shook her head. "You can't tell her that. It's simply not true!"

He grinned. "I know it, but it's the only thing that will work."

"I won't tell. I promise to the moon and back and all around the stars."

"Then we better get moving. We have to stop at the boarding house for our things afterwards. Are you up to moving in tonight?"

"Yes! Yes!" Chelsea began jumping around. They left and went to the eatery, where Charlie Baxter had already known Brent had rented a house from the pastor.

"I rented less than two hours ago and everyone knows," he told Sam.

She laughed. "Welcome to Cooper's Ridge, where everyone knows your business before you do."

Chapter 7

Brent dropped off Chelsea at school and walked over to the sheriff's office. Luckily, Sheriff Mac was there. He fixed his shirt and walked up the steps, careful not to make any noise. If he changed his mind when he got to the door, then he could high-tail it out of there before anyone saw him.

The sheriff waved at him through the large window. Too late to turn and flee now. He wasn't about to be known as a yellow belly. Brent opened the door and walked inside. Before the sheriff could say a word, he cleared his throat and spoke. "I'll take that job you offered as deputy."

Sheriff Mac stood and watched Brent, assessing him from head to toe. "Well, son, I'd suggest you find a change of clothes and a pair of real cowboy boots and stop by before I close today. That'll give you time to pick up Chelsea and make arrangements for her to stay with someone while you're working."

"You mean I can't bring her along with me to work?"

"No, sir. A sheriff's office is no place for a child. Nor is it for a deputy in training. I only need you three evenings a week from five in the afternoon until ten or so. After ten, you can be on call. If someone needs you they'll come knocking on your door. We'll take turns. I'm also keeping my current deputy so if he fails to show up, you'll have to. Can you handle the job?"

"I told you I'll take it when I walked in here. A few more stipulations won't bother me."

"Good. I like a man who is precise and is up for a challenge. See you at five sharp. My wife is making chicken and dumplings and I plan to sit down and sup with her for once."

"Thanks for the opportunity."

The sheriff eyed him, then nodded. "I believe you are a man of honor or I'd never have asked you to take the job. To me your trying to find a place to call home. Maybe this job will help."

Brent was happy to get the job but he didn't know what to do with Chelsea. He hadn't left her alone since Sallie left, scared she'd be afraid to stay alone. She was too young to stay by herself even though he had when he was her age. But that was different. He was a boy. She was his precious daughter.

An idea occurred to him. He stopped in at the book store and found Sam. She swung around with a pile of books in her arms. He took them from her and asked her where to place them.

"Over there," she pointed. "What are you doing here so early, Brent? It's not time for class. Besides, today's class is in the evening."

"I'm afraid I have to cancel this evening's class. Maybe all of them."

She followed him, stopping abruptly when he got to the table where he laid the books down carefully.

"Brent? I'm so disappointed in you. Just because Chelsea goes to school, you don't care about learning to read?"

He laughed. "Don't get so upset, Sam. I got a job!" He swung around to watch her reaction.

"You did? First you rented a house and now you got a job? Does this mean your not going on an adventure any longer? Will you be staying in Cooper's Ridge permanently?"

He shrugged. "I don't know. I'm going to give it a good shot and see how it works out without promising anything. I want the best for Chelsea."

She laid a hand on his arm. "You should also want the best for yourself, Brent."

He shook his head. "I don't deserve it. But she does and I'm going to make sure she is happy. Twice, she had mothers walk away from her. I won't allow it to happen again."

"Twice?" Sam was confused at first until she realized he meant Chelsea's birth mother abandoned her.

"We told her that her real mother died and went to heaven. We don't know what happened to her except she left the child on the steps of the orphanage in Dallas to either be saved or die. Either way, the mother never came back for her. She lived in the orphanage for six years until we came along. Then Sallie up and left her, too."

"Is that why you really went on an adventure with her? To see where the two of you belong?"

He nodded. "Something like that."

She smiled. "If you think you're getting away with not coming to class in the evenings because you have a job now, I'm making a special class for you right now. Have a seat and we'll get started."

"You'd do that for me? Change your whole schedule around?"

"You seem shocked. Of course I would. Do you know why, Brent? Because you are worth it."

He sat down and she sat in the seat beside him, then opened a book. "Are you ready?"

"Wait! I have to go check with Miss Rachel to see if she can take Chelsea while I am working? I can't leave her alone and the sheriff said as a deputy I don't need to have a child there."

Sam smiled. "I would love her company, Brent. She can be dropped off with me and we'll study and have supper together. If you'd like me to take her home and get her ready for bed, I can do that, too. Otherwise, you can pick her up here when you leave work. Not here, but upstairs. There is a side entrance to my apartment."

"Everything is happening at once."

"Let it happen, Brent. It's all for the good. You are where God wants you to be."

"What I can't figure out is why he wasn't there eleven months ago when Sallie up and left a child without a mother."

"You can't blame God for that. We all have our own journey to take. What happens is part of building our character."

"You wouldn't say that if you'd seen the pure heartbreak in the child's eyes."

She patted his hand again. This time he caught it in his. "I like you, Sam. I'm trying to make things work here. I want to kiss you right here, right now. But it complicates everything. Chelsea has to come first."

"I'd have it no other way." She pulled her hand back. "I'm probably complicating things for you. I'm sorry, Brent. There are things I have to work out, too."

He shook his head. "You? You look like a woman who has it all together, even when you are wearing britches."

They both laughed. "Especially when I'm wearing britches," she told him.

"Maybe so. Thanks, Sam. I really hope this works out and we can stay here. I just don't want Chelsea hurt again."

"Do you think her mother will ever look for her?"

He shook his head. "Sallie? I doubt it. She used me for my money, I'm aware of that now. I've put back a pretty nice nest egg from my gambling days. If she hadn't spent half of it, we'd be good for a lot longer."

"Do you need some help? I have some extra. It isn't much, but if it helps Chelsea, I don't mind helping."

Brent put up a hand. "You don't understand, Sam. I have enough money put back that Chelsea and I are able to travel anywhere we want and live quite nicely for a long, long time. I'm choosing to work. There's no way I can be idle and it's good for the soul. The extra pay will be put away in the bank for her someday."

"Thank God! I really didn't want to give up my savings!"

Brent laughed. He took two fingers and lifted her chin. "How I want to kiss your lips, sweet lady."

"A customer may walk in," she told him but it didn't sound as if she cared one way or another.

He leaned in and placed a soft, sweet kiss on her mouth.

She allowed the kiss and then playfully pushed him away. "Let's get started." Sam opened the book again since she had accidentally closed it when he kissed her.

They spent the better part of an hour working on his reading skills until the doctor's wife and the sheriff's sister came in and needed Sam's help with books. Brent left quietly and promised to bring Chelsea back before he went to work.

*****

Sam was thrilled she'd get some time with Chelsea this evening. Meanwhile, she had two customers to take care of.

The ladies spent almost another hour browsing the books and asking questions and suggestions for books to read. Marie, who was married to Doc Owen, looked around and sighed. "We'd love to be able to sit here and chat with other ladies. This is a nice book store."

An idea was forming in Sam's mind. "Would you ladies be interested in joining a book club?"

"What is a book club? How does it work?"

"I'm not sure, but why can't we make up our own rules?"

"That would be delightful."

For the next twenty minutes Marie and Winnie helped Sam plan a new club, which they were officially starting next Wednesday afternoon. "I'll close the store one hour early each Wednesday. That way it doesn't interfere with anyone's evening plans."

She was actually thinking about Chelsea and having to keep her in the evenings while Brent was being a deputy. She wanted Chelsea all to herself and didn't plan to share her with a room full of ladies. Otherwise, she'd rather have the club in the evening. No matter, it was another opportunity to build her book store.

One of the ladies had a great idea. "We can take turns reading a chapter or two out loud each week until the book is finished. There's also a new bakery in town. I'll drop by and purchase some sweet delights for us."

"That's generous of you, Marie."

Winnie spoke up, too. "I'll bring a pitcher of my lemonade. Cordie will want to be a part of this club too. You know, the sheriff's sister? She married Joseph from the furniture store. Do you think we should charge a book club membership fee to cover any expenses that may occur?"

Sam shook her head. "This is a wonderful opportunity for every woman to get a small break from their busy lives and to encourage reading. This will have to be a free service the book store is offering, since I'm sure some ladies can't afford to pay a membership fee."

"We certainly don't want you to compromise your store in any way to pull this off. Why don't we find a way to raise money for the club without taking any of its profits?"

Sam loved the idea! "That will be fun, ladies. I can't wait until our first meeting."

Marie and Winnie gave her a hug. "We're so happy for you, Sam. I love having a book store in Cooper's Ridge."

The ladies left and Sam was so excited. She was so busy searching for the perfect book for their first meeting next week, she forgot to close the shop at three. An hour later, Chelsea showed up with her father.

"My goodness, the time has flown by this afternoon!" She greeted the two and Brent handed her a basket that had a delicious aroma coming from underneath the cloth that covered it.

"What is this?"

"I stopped by Charlie Baxter's eatery and brought us some soup and fresh baked bread for supper. It's the least I can do for watching Chelsea for me while I'm at work."

"Can we stay in the store all night and look at books?"

Sam gave her attention to Chelsea's request. "We'll have to go to my place after a while, but for now, why don't we take a seat at the table in the back of the store and have some soup?"

"Yummy! I'm so hungry!" Chelsea hopped to the table and sat down, talking about her first day at school.

Brent spoke up. "Young lady. Please ask Sam where you can wash your hands before we sit at the table."

Chelsea had been so excited to be eating with Sam she had forgotten. Her face fell and she looked worried. Sam motioned for her and her father to follow her to the back of the store where she kept a basin filled with water for hand washing and cleaning up.

They finished with that and sat at the table to eat. After Brent said grace, they all dug in, laughing and talking the whole time. Sam was filled with a feeling of family more than she'd ever known in her whole life. Was this what it would be like to have a real family?

The warmth and joy that had entered the room was something that was new to her. Right before he left, Brent leaned over and kissed her on the cheek. She watched as he walked down the street towards the Sheriff's office, her hand over the cheek where he placed the kiss.

Was she falling for this man?

Or, was he just being a nice man who needed someone to help him with Chelsea?

Chapter 8

Sam had been keeping Chelsea a few evenings a week for the past two and a half weeks. They were becoming so close and she loved being with the young girl. They spent so much time learning to read but Sam didn't mind at all. The girl was learning quickly. Between school and time in the book store, Chelsea was picking up much faster than Sam had imagined.

Her book store had a lot of traffic on certain days and the weekly women's book club was so much fun that she was surprised when the end of the month had arrived. "I can't believe it's almost July. June flew by so fast," she mentioned to one of her customers.

The woman turned around and smiled. "Did you forget that we planned to go to the bakery? How about today?"

Pastor Murphy's wife, Catherine, was so beautiful. She had dark hair and tiny features, but held her head in such a way that Sam knew she was a strong and proud woman. There were age lines at her eyes that told of a long, hard life. Yet her smile was angelic and Sam knew she was a woman who had learned many lessons in life.

"I'd love to. As a matter of fact, Catherine, have you heard about our women's book club?"

"I did and several ladies have invited me. Perhaps someday things will slow down for me enough that I can join, but not yet."

"You are always welcome," Sam told her. She turned the sign on the door to closed and locked it in case someone stumbled onto the porch and didn't read that she was closed. It was about one o'clock in the afternoon and she usually ate as she worked so it wasn't necessary to close the shop. But today it would be nice to get out.

"Thank you. There is so much to be done for the ministry and Cooper deserves to have an attentive wife by his side. I managed to get away today as he in Mill Ridge and I stayed here so you and I can have some time together."

That was nice of the pastor's wife, but Sam was confused why spending time with her was so important to Catherine. After all, they only knew each other in passing or from church socials. "Thanks for inviting me. This is a nice break from my daily routine."

"Of course. I'm sure you are wondering why and we'll discuss that as soon as we get to the bakery."

Sam didn't like that. Had she done something wrong? A hand touched her sleeve. "Please don't worry, it's nothing you've done."

"I'm so glad. You had me worried for a moment, Catherine. You hold a lot of weight in this town and I don't want to upset the apple cart, as they say."

Catherine gave her a huge smile and tucked her arm in Sam's. They chatted as they walked until they got to the bakery.

"How lovely," Catherine mentioned. "Would you like to sit outside? They put some tables and chairs right in front of the bakery."

Sam agreed. "That would be so nice. We can watch people as they go by."

Catherine laughed. "I love people watching. Shh, don't tell a soul I said that, I'll deny it. When I lived at the farm, I'd go visit Nora White at the ranch and we'd laugh and watch the cowboy hands and workers coming and going. It was fun. I do have to go visit her soon. Perhaps you'd like to ride along next time I go?"

"I'm sure I can if I'm not busy with the book store. Just let me know."

"Wonderful. I'll make plans and give you plenty of warning. Let's go inside and pick something delicious to enjoy."

While they were choosing a dessert, Sam wondered why Catherine was so interested in spending so much time with her. Things didn't seem right, but maybe that's how the woman was. After all, Sam had always been too busy working at the livery and painting her book store to bother with anyone on a personal level.

Now that she was a dignified business woman, had that made a difference in how people saw her?

"What if I get the chocolate custard and you get the apple crisp? Then we can split it and share."

"Good idea. Let's do it," Sam agreed. She loved trying out new things.

They went outside to sit while the proprietor brought them coffee first, then their desserts. Sam and Catherine were laughing and tasting each other's dessert.

At one point the sheriff rode by on his gelding. "Howdy, Catherine. Sam! That looks mighty tasty."

"It is, Sheriff," Catherine called out. "Now don't' go telling my husband you caught me here. He's bringing me some apple dumplings from Mill Ridge today. I plan on having them for dessert this evening, too."

He tipped his hat and moved on. Sam finished her dessert, then wiped her mouth. "Catherine, is there a reason I'm here? I have to be honest. This is highly unusual for me to be invited somewhere, especially by the town's owner's wife."

Catherine took the last bite of her dessert, then a sip of coffee. She wiped her mouth on a napkin that had been sitting on her lap and clasped both hands in front of her while holding the napkin. "You are right, Sam. You are a bright young lady and don't fool easy.

I was contemplating how I want to start this conversation, so I shall just begin."

"I don't understand."

"When are you going to tell him?"

Sam froze. There was only one person in all of Cooper's Ridge that she was holding a secret from. Her father. "Is this a wild guess or do you know something that I don't?" Sam bit her lip. If she placed any more pressure on it, she'd make it bleed.

Her hands got sweaty and her throat was so constricted that Sam was barely able to speak when Catherine leaned in. "You know exactly what I'm talking about and I don't want to say it in case someone walks by and hears us before you announce the truth. The reason I brought you here is to find out why you haven't come forward and talked to him yet?"

"I don't know."

"I think you do," she said softly. Catherine was a nice lady. She always treated Sam with respect and kindness. Right now there was a look in her eyes that told Sam she needed to face this.

Sam stared into her eyes, which were filled with apathy. "I'm not sure. I'm afraid."

"And I am afraid that if you don't tell him, you will be stripping him of this new opportunity. I don't mean to be disrespectful of your mother, but why didn't she ever tell him?"

"That was impossible. She died when I was about six years old. I don't know anything before that. Maybe she tried to find him, I'm not sure. Perhaps he knows." She deliberately avoided using his name as a few townsfolk walked by.

A hand came across the table and rested on top of Sam's. "I'm so sorry, Sam. Is that why you grew up in an orphanage?"

She nodded, not wanting to remember that horrible day when they told her that her mother was dead. "At least I had the orphanage. So many times I wanted to run away and try to find my mother, but they said she was dead and I didn't even know what dead meant. When I learned about death and understood she was never coming back, I tried to be a good orphan. But there was always a wild side of me that made me wonder who my father was."

Catherine smiled. "I can see that. The first day I looked at you wearing those men's britches and acting all tough and unladylike-like, it felt familiar. It took me months to figure it out. That's why I'm here. I'm surprised no one else has realized you have your father's eyes along with his brash personality and foolish bravery."

"Foolish bravery? That doesn't sound very nice," she pushed back.

Catherine gave her hand another pat. "I don't mean that in any way but positive, dear. Like your father, you take chances. Look at you. What made you come halfway across the nation to find him? I'd say you are quite brave and yet foolish for making your way alone."

"I had a disguise. It worked up until Noel, Kansas."

Catherine was silent for a few moments. "Our teacher, Miss Molly and Harrison were your travel associates. Do they know?"

Sam sighed. She didn't want Molly to be looked upon as anything but the delightful woman she was. "I asked Molly not to mention it until I figured it all out. I wanted to tell him so many times."

"Stop wasting time, Sam. You both deserve to get to know each other. He deserves to know."

"I'll try."

"Now, let's enjoy the walk back." They left the bakery and walked arm in arm back to the book store. Catherine gave her a hug first, then a long look. "My husband will be returning from Mill Ridge later this afternoon. You are welcome to stop by this evening if you'd like."

Sam didn't have Chelsea this evening and there wasn't any classes to attend to. Tonight would be the best time to confront her father. She nodded. "I'll try."

*****

Chelsea was running down the street towards the book store faster than Brent was able to keep up. She was so excited that her book report got a good marking, the first person she wanted to tell was Sam.

"Father, I have to tell Sam. Can we stop there before we go home?"

She barely had time to get the question out when he nodded and she took off like a flock of roosters were chasing her. It was a good day, Brent thought and hurried to keep up with her.

Luckily, the book store was still open. He pulled out his stop watch and glanced at the time, which was ten minutes until three when the store closed for the day.

The bell above the door jangled to announce them. As Sam turned to greet them, her eyes were red and she looked a bit pale. He knew something had happened, but what was wrong?

Chelsea was so excited about the good grade, she was jumping up and down in front of her. Sam tried to contain herself, he could see her forcing a smile. "I'm so proud of you, Chelsea," Sam told the child and gave her a hug.

"I'm going to be the best student in the whole class," she told Sam. "Willy said he is but I'm going to read so many books that he won't be able to keep up with me!"

"I'm sure you already are the best reader in the class. I'm proud of you."

"Thank you," she remembered to say. "Can I get another book, Father?"

"Yes. Go ahead and choose one, Chelsea." The child ran to the children's section to leaf through the many books there.

Brent turned back to Sam. "What happened? Are you all right?"

"I'm not sure what you mean," she told him.

"You appear distraught and that worries me."

"I'm fine, really." She sighed. "Remember when I told you that I have some things to work out?"

He nodded, then waited for her to continue.

"This is one of them. I have to work something out this evening."

He tilted his head to the side and watched her. Sam tried to hide her emotions but he saw right through it. "Is this something I can help you with?"

"I'd rather not say. Not yet."

"I understand." He didn't, really. "Would you like to have supper with Chelsea and I?"

"I can't. I'm having supper somewhere else."

"I see. Okay. I'll be at home. Chelsea and I are having supper and watching the stars later on when it gets dark. A quiet evening together."

"That's wonderful, Brent. A father should spend time with his daughter."

Her voice cracked and she almost let out a sob. He was really concerned. "Sam? You're not okay. Tell me what's going on?"

She shook her head. " Not now. I promise if I have any trouble, you will be the first person I seek out."

"Promise?"

"Yes."

"You can pinky-swear," Chelsea told them, walking towards the two with a new book in her hand.

Sam smiled even though he could see the pain in her eyes. "That's silly," she told Chelsea.

"No, it's not." Chelsea sounded like a grown adult. She showed Sam how to pinky-swear and they giggled. Then she looked at her father. "You have to pinky-swear, Father."

He lifted his hand and took Sam's pinky with his. She looked at him with glazed over eyes and he said, "Ready. Do you pinky-swear to find me if you need me?"

"I pinky-swear," she told him, halfway between laughing and sobbing.

He pulled her close, not caring about anything or anyone who would see them. "I'm going to hold you to that," he whispered in her ear.

She pulled back and tried hard to contain herself. There was something horribly wrong. Brent didn't want to leave her alone until Sam insisted.

"You should go. I have to close the shop and be on my way."

"Can we walk you somewhere?" He was still trying to find out what was going on without intruding on her privacy.

She shook her head. "No, you can't. Now, go home, Brent."

"Bye, Sam. I love you." Chelsea grabbed her skirts and gave them a hug.

Sam tousled the top of her hair. "Bye, Chelsea. I love you, too. Have a good night with your father."

"I will! I will!" she repeated, then was out the door.

*****

Sam stood at the window, looking out until she turned the sign to closed. Taking a deep breath, she walked out of the book store and went upstairs for a few moments. Catherine said her husband would be home late afternoon. It was late afternoon.

It was time to tell him exactly who she was.

Fear of rejection came over her and she stumbled across the floor and flung herself onto her bed. She was finding it impossible to step outside and walk to the church where she was sure he was at right now. Either there or at their home where she had an open invitation to visit.

Several minutes later, she pulled herself together, washed her face and pinched her cheeks.

Sam turned and walked out of her apartment.

Samantha the orphan had reared up and tried to take over like the ugly evil it was. She squelched that demon and pushed it down as far as it would go.

Sam the book lady walked down the street, ready to confront her past.

No matter what, she still had her dignity. She knew who she was and where she belonged.

Sam just hoped she'd still be welcome in Cooper's Ridge tomorrow.

Chapter 9

The church looked intimidating. Usually when a person steps inside the church, there is an illusion of warmth and love. Sam felt nothing close to that as she walked through the huge door of the building and into the empty room.

There was dead silence in the sanctuary. When the door shut, the noise from outside of wagons moving down the street or people crunching boots on the boardwalk stopped.

Total silence was awful. She wanted to turn and run out the front door like the coward she was. Sam had to sit down for a few minutes. She walked to the front of the church, her new kid boots the only sound in the entire place.

As she slid into the front pew, she closed her eyes and took in a deep breath. This was not easy. She had to make some kind of noise. Was God here? Would he listen?

Pastor Murphy's home was right beside the church but she wanted to stop here first. She saw a dim light in the window even though it wasn't dark yet. Two people were sitting at the table talking as she walked by and she knew it was Catherine and her father.

Father.

She didn't dare call him that. Not yet. Not until he allowed her to. Why was it so hard to tell him he had a daughter? Would he want her? The pastor was a nice man. He was always so good to her.

Would he still be when he found out?

She looked at the cross at the front of the church. *God, you have to know if he will accept me. My father is a preacher. He loves you.*

Will you soften his heart so he can love me, too? I'm an adult and yet I yearn for a man that I never knew as my father. Your love shining down should be enough. Help me, Lord. Show me what to do.

Sam waited but there was no answer. Which of course she knew there wouldn't be any. God had his own way of showing her the way. It had been like that all of her life. Something had propelled her to leave New York City the moment she left the orphanage.

Was everything that happened in the last year leading to this moment?

Thinking back, she ran through every trial and tribulation she had gone through from the time she walked out of the orphanage.

She stood and walked to the front of the church, then kneeled in front of the cross and spoke out loud. "What if I don't tell him? Perhaps only I should be the one to know. Does he even need to know that I am his daughter? He has a good life here and helps people all the time. God, you have gifted him with blessings to make this town come alive. He doesn't need me. He does not need me. I can't do this."

"It's not your fault."

The soft spoken words behind her caught Sam off guard. She turned to see Pastor Murphy, her father, walking slowly down the isle. He kneeled beside her like the calm gentleman she knew.

"Whatever happened to you can be forgiven. Have you forgiven the ones who hurt you, Sam?"

"You have no idea of what you are saying, sir."

"It doesn't matter. Shall we pray?"

She kept quiet while he said the Lord's Prayer and then talked about forgiveness and a few other things. Sam wasn't paying attention any longer. Her father had taken her hand and its warmth reminded her that she still hadn't told him who she was.

She wanted to run. The pastor thought he was helping one of his members ease their pain and suffering. He had no idea this was about him.

Sam still had the opportunity to keep quiet and never say a word. Something inside of her prompted her to let it out.

Her voice was a soft whisper. "My mother was Josephine Corta Malone."

She felt him stiffen beside her. "Josie? From New York City? She is your mother?"

Sam nodded. She was afraid to look at him to see his reaction since she knew how confused he had to be. Then a power of strength came over her that she hadn't expected. "She was my mother and you, sir, are my father."

"What? Your father? It can't be? I haven't seen her in twenty years."

Sam shook her head. "I'm almost twenty."

"Where is she? She needs to explain this nonsense instead of sending you here. Why did you wait so long to tell me?" He sounded confused, angry. He was a preacher. Was he supposed to behave this way?

It worried Sam that she'd be hated for something her mother failed to do. She had always promised Sam she'd change her life and they'd find her father. She remembered that as much as she did her mother's face. But she wasn't going to be punished for something her mother failed to do. "It's not nonsense. My mother is dead. She can't tell you anything." Sam stood.

He held up a hand and then stood up, looking her dead in the eye. "Sam, I like you a lot. I knew there was something that you were hiding but I never wanted to mind your business. You told me when you came that your past was not going to ruin your future here in Cooper's Ridge. That was a requirement of living here."

"What? I can't believe you just said that! I'm telling you that you are my father and all you're worried about is the fact that I lied about my past interfering in my future here in Cooper's Ridge. You are so full of yourself."

She didn't realize her voice had risen until he lifted a hand. "I'm sorry, Sam. You're right. This is all a shock. Are you sure that your mother told you the truth? She was a - lady of -"

"Ill repute? I know what she was. When I was fifteen, Sister Elaine Catherine told me everything."

"Why didn't your mother tell you?"

"She died when I was six."

"Six. Dear Lord, I'm so sorry, Sam."

"Don't be sorry. I made out just fine."

He shook his head. "No, you didn't. You went to an orphanage." He turned away from her then and she felt as if he couldn't look at her any longer. It was time to go. This was turning out exactly like she thought it would. She heard rejection over and over again in her head. There was nothing more he could say or do to make up for all the years she spent in an orphanage when she had a father perfectly capable of raising her.

She should be the one angry, not him. Sam reached up and pulled on the chain at her neck. She walked over to her father and handed him the locket.

His eyes widened. He held it in his hand. She knew that he was fully aware of what photo was inside the locket. It was a photo of her mother and him.

"She asked Sister Elaine Catherine to make sure I got the locket. She dropped me off at the orphanage a few weeks before she died. You can't deny that is not your face. She told the Sister who the father was. Now you know. There's nothing more for you to do."

Sam walked away from him, not expecting any further reaction. He'd already shown that he had no interest in a daughter. This was why she hadn't wanted to tell him.

She walked out of the church and down the street, not really paying attention to where she was going. Sam made her way to the livery, snuck in the side door and spent time with the horses. She brushed two and then felt like she was suffocating in the barn.

As she walked down the street, Sam realized it was dark. Brent and Chelsea were out on the porch star gazing. She stopped and asked if she could sit with them. Brent took her hand and nodded, making room for her to sit beside him.

She wasn't able to talk, and luckily Chelsea had gotten so tired, she was leaning against Brent's chest and hanging her head. Slowly her eyes closed, and she fell asleep.

He stood up with Chelsea in his arms. "I'll be right back," he said, his voice low so he wouldn't wake up the sleeping child.

Sam stared up at the sky, thinking how in awe she'd always been watching the stars and moon. They had looked so far away and she always dreamed that someday she'd follow the stars and it would lead her to her father.

She heard the front door close. Brent sat down beside her and picked up her hand, holding it softly in his. He didn't speak, just waited patiently for her to talk when she was ready.

She watched the stars for a while then laid her head against his shoulder. He put an arm around her shoulders and sighed. "I'm listening," he said, his tone so low that it didn't break the serene mood.

"I came to Cooper's Ridge because my father is here. I never met him. He didn't know I exist. Now he does."

Brent pulled her closer, making it easier to talk to him. "I love you, Sam. You don't have to say a word. Just know that I do."

She laid a hand on his cheek. "Thank you, Brent. Your words mean so much to me. I believe I feel the same way but I'm so full of emotions right now I can't think."

"You don't have to. I know you care for me and that's all I ask. We can figure it all out later. Right now, it's about you and your father."

They sat together for the longest time until a shadow came down the street. The booted heels made a clunking noise on the boardwalk. When they walked past Brent's porch, the booted sound stopped, then he turned and walked to the porch. "Sam?" His voice sounded tired, sympathetic.

She sniffed, not sure she even wanted to speak to him. She sat up straight and looked at Brent. "Meet my father, Pastor Murphy."

Brent was quiet. She didn't blame him. Everyone in town would be shocked when they found out. If she stuck around long enough for them to find out. Except she knew this town and everyone would know by morning that she was the daughter of the town's founder.

"We have to talk, Sam. I overreacted. I'm sorry." He held out his hand that held her necklace. "I gave this to your mother. It's meant for you to have."

She reached out and took it from him, sorry that she had tried to throw it away like that.

Brent patted her shoulder and then stood. "If you'll excuse me, I'll be inside. Pastor Murphy, Sam." He went inside, closing the door behind him.

Pastor Murphy came up on the porch.

"Sit down," she told him, wanting to talk things out. She hated the idea that she ran off like a child. "I'm sorry for the way I reacted, too."

"I don't blame you. Catherine came in when she saw you running down the street and gave me a lecture that could fill up a month of Sundays."

Sam gave him a sad smile. "Catherine is great."

"She's a lifesaver and has been the love of my life."

"Tell me about my mother. I remember her talks to me how she was going to get better and take me to meet you. She had promised me over and over and then she died."

"I'm sorry. If I had known, perhaps my life would've been different, too. Back then, there was no way I'd have been a good father. I was a bounty hunter, trying to catch the bad men in the world. Even if your mother had told me, I don't know how I would've reacted back in those days. I was pretty wild then."

"I was only six, but I do remember she said you were born to roam the west, catching bad men and doing good all over. She told me that someday we'd meet up with you. I always believed her until she died."

"Will you forgive me, Sam? For not being there for you all these years? I promise to make it up to you now that I know who you really are."

She cried. Not just a few sobs and dropped tears. No, she cried like a baby, tears rolling down her cheeks and her body shaking like a little newborn lamb caught in the rain.

Cooper Murphy gathered his long lost daughter in his arms. "I'll be here for you for the rest of my life," he vowed.

"I believe you," she told him between sobs. Brent came outside, closing the door softly behind him. He waited silently in the shadows, there if Sam needed him.

"Everything is okay now, Brent. I feel free to love you."

Cooper Murphy let go of his daughter and motioned for Brent to come closer. He grabbed Brent's shoulder. "We're all getting to know each other right now, but I think you're a good man. Either way, I'll be keeping an eye on you."

The clip-clop of horse's hooves echoed through the quiet streets. Everyone looked up when the stage came in this late. "I didn't know we were getting a stage this time of the evening," the pastor said out loud.

"Maybe it was late coming in," Brent replied.

"Whoever it is, a beautiful woman just got out. It's hard to see with the dim lamp the driver is holding up, but she has the reddest hair I've ever seen on a woman."

Brent moved to the front of the porch. "Red hair?"

Sam sniffed, wiped her cheeks and nodded. She looked at Brent to see a hardened, angry look on his face.

"Do you know her?" Sam asked, not thinking much about the question.

"Yes. I never thought I'd see her again."

"Oh? Who is she?" A terribly bad feeling began to rise at the way Brent kept staring at the stage and that woman.

"That's Sallie. My wife."

Chapter 10

Brent stood watching to see what Sallie was going to do. What did she want? He knew one thing without a doubt and that was that she didn't want him or Chelsea, so what was she doing here of all places? How did she even know they were here? He looked at Sam and saw the confused, distraught look on her face.

Just when everything was going right. Sam found her father and got all of that worked out, realizing there was room in her life for him. He knew they were going to take it slow but that was okay. He knew that Sam was the one he wanted for the rest of his life. He was falling in love again and trying to settle down in one spot and then a part of his past shows up in the middle of the night.

Not a good part of his life either. Sallie had hurt him and Chelsea badly.

He heard the door open. It had a small creak in it that he meant to fix. "Father, are you here? I can't sleep." Chelsea came out on the porch rubbing her eyes with both hands.

When she found her father, he lifted her into his arms. He was hoping to get her back inside before she saw Sallie. The girl did not need to be hurt again. It had broken his heart to see her cry for weeks after Sallie up and left without saying goodbye. No, he wasn't going to allow her to come strolling back in like she was the belle of the ball. He had to find out what she was doing here first.

"Sam, would you mind helping Chelsea back inside? I really need to find out why our guest is here." He was hoping she understood what he was doing and Sam stood and held her arms open for Chelsea.

"Chelsea, I am so tired. How about I go with you and read a story to you? Would you like that?" She nodded and clung to Sam's neck.

Thank you," Brent told her.

Sam sighed and went inside, the door making its usual noise. He had to get rid of Sallie before she ruined everything.

Pastor Murphy finally spoke up. "Who is Sallie?"

"I was married to her and we adopted Chelsea from the Orphan Train. I thought I told you my story when I first got here."

The pastor shook his head. "No. You just said you wanted to take Chelsea on an adventure. I'm heading home. I'm sure Catherine is wanting to know how everything went. Let me know if you need any help with this situation. We don't allow no falderal in this town, you know."

"I understand." Brent left the porch behind the pastor and headed in the opposite direction towards the stage. He heard the driver tell Sallie he was taking the horses to the livery overnight and would be ready to leave at eight in the morning. Hopefully, that meant she wasn't staying around long.

Brent didn't need her complicating his life. Not now when things were finally working out. He decided to get this over with. "Sallie!"

She turned, her beautiful porcelain skin and blue eyes staring at him. "Brent."

He stopped in front of her. "Where's your gambler? The one you ran off with and gave up everything that I thought made you happy?"

"You sound bitter and I don't blame you, Brent."

"You'd best leave here. Chelsea is finally settling down and not crying hysterically for you any longer."

The words cut through to her as he looked into her blue eyes and saw the guilt there. Still, she had no rights anymore. She abandoned them and the courts agreed. His divorce was granted almost immediately.

"I didn't want to hurt her. I'm truly sorry about that, Brent. I came here to find you and that's why I insisted on having the stage bring me in so late. I did not want Chelsea to see me. I hope she is fast asleep."

He shook his head. "She's not. She almost saw you but luckily she's back in her bed. What do you want?"

She opened her reticule and pulled out an envelope. "I was going to give this to you tomorrow but I have to leave with the stage by eight in the morning. You know how mornings are for me." She smiled as if she were telling a joke.

There was nothing funny about her at all. Sallie had her chance with him. Now all he wanted was her out of his life and his daughter's life.

She held out the envelope. "This is for you."

"What is it?" He didn't take it.

"I owe you this money. I scored big, Brent. I mean big! I hit the jackpot several times and now I'm heading to California so you don't have to worry about ever seeing me again. But I knew I couldn't go until I sought your forgiveness. I did you and Chelsea wrong and I'm so sorry."

At least she was apologizing, which was a complete surprise coming from a selfish person like Sallie. He didn't know how sincere she was but he had to admit she did come out of her way to find him. "How did you know I was here?"

"You sent a telegram to your banker last week to move your accounts here. Harold is my cousin. He told me."

"Something as simple as that." He shook his head.

Miss Rachel came out on her porch. "Are you in need of a room for the night?"

Sallie turned and waved. "Yes, ma'am. I'll be right there." She turned back to Brent and lifted her hand to his cheek. "The money means nothing to me, Brent. You make sure you spend it on Chelsea. I'm sorry. I hope you have a good life."

*****

Sam tucked Chelsea in and went back outside onto the porch. She looked around for Brent and saw him in the middle of the street with that woman. His wife. A sob escaped her. As Sam watched, she lifted her hand to his face and then turned away.

Then Brent called out to her. "I forgive you," he told her and she walked back to him and gave him a hug. He held her in his arms and Sam couldn't take any more. She hurried down the street, desperate to get to her apartment and shut out the world. What she saw just broke her heart.

How could Brent take a woman like that back? How could he love her after what she did to him and Chelsea?

She was almost at her door when a hand fell onto her shoulder. She swung around, ready to defend herself when she saw Brent's face in front of her.

"Let me be," she told him, trying to turn the knob to get inside.

"Sam, stop. It's not what you think. I don't love her. It's you I love."

"It didn't look that way to me, Brent. Just leave me alone."

He swung her around and pulled her to him, then bent his head and kissed her so hard, she was breathless. He let her go and whispered, "I'm going to marry you, book lady. Wait and see." Then he turned and left her standing there.

Two months later

Pastor Murphy threw his fist in the air and gave out the loudest hoot the town of Cooper's Ridge had ever heard. He was so darn happy these days.

"Father, you're embarrassing me," Sam told him. "I'm the one that's supposed to be so happy since it's my wedding day."

He twirled her around and gave out another hoot, then addressed the congregation who had witnessed the wedding of the pastor's daughter. "I want to thank everyone here for being here today. It means the world to me. For twenty long years I didn't know this young woman existed. When I found out, I was angry that she hadn't told me after living in this town for almost a year.

Then I realized we all have things we don't want to talk about or reveal. There are reasons for keeping secrets but I'm glad she finally came out with the truth. I wasn't perfect in my younger years and I'll be the first to admit it. Now, let's celebrate love and life and joy and God. Everyone, meet my beautiful daughter and my new son. Now, let's have a celebration!"

The crowd applauded while Brent and Sam made their way to the front of the church. Sam took Chelsea's hand and pulled her along down the aisle. Chelsea tugged at her arm.

Sam stopped and leaned down. "What is it, Chelsea?"

"Can I call you Mother?"

Sam almost cried right there in the middle of the sanctuary. She got down on her knee and prayed the dress wouldn't tear but she wasn't too concerned. This was way more important. "Yes, Chelsea, you may call me mother as long as I may call you daughter."

Chelsea began to jump up and down again, her pony tails bobbing and her new glasses falling down her nose. She took a finger and pushed them back up and began to laugh. Her arms went around Sam's neck and she hugged her tight. "Mother," she whispered. "I'm so glad you're my mother."

Brent leaned down to help Sam up. "What am I missing here?" he asked. Sam and Chelsea looked at each other and began to giggle. He laughed and held out his arms. Chelsea, who was in the middle, reached for her father's hand first, then her mother's hand. They left the church, the three of them a united family.

Sam stood on the steps outside and looked up at the perfect blue sky. "I never thought an orphan like me would find this much happiness."

Brent kissed her cheek. "I'm glad we found each other."

"And me. I was an orphan too. Now I'm like Sam, I mean Mother."

Brent and Sam looked at Chelsea, her smile so wide Sam thought it would stretch her mouth to her ears. "Like me?" Sam asked.

"Yes. Just like you. I'm filled with this much happiness." She opened her arms wide and lifted her sweet face to the sky. "Can we go home now?"

"Let's go home," Sam said, tucking her arm through Brent's.

"Home it is," he said, kissing her sweet lips in front of everyone who stood outside. "I love you, Sam."

"And me too. You love me too, right Father?"

Sam and Brent roared with laughter. "I love you too, Sunshine. Let's go home."

Thank you for reading The Bookworm. The next book is available now on Amazon & Kindle Unlimited!

THE LITTLE BAKER

[1](https://www.amazon.com/gp/product/B0B5BFHT9D)

In the meantime, feel free to go to www.cyndiraye.com[2] for a free novella when you sign up to be on my reader's exclusive list.

Have you read all of the Outlaws & Orphans books? Keep turning he page to find a free chapter of The Runaway, book 1 of the series.

---

1. https://www.amazon.com/gp/product/B0B5BFHT9D

2. http://www.cyndiraye.com

Free Chapter of The Runaway

The Runaway Free Chapter
Chapter 1

Cooper's Ridge, Texas

Pastor Murphy nodded to his congregation. "Good Morning, folks. I'm going to step aside for a few minutes as one of our neighbors, Olivia Young, the founding member of the Orphan Train Committee , has an announcement to make." The preacher stood back and motioned for the young woman to rise. "Come front and center."

Owen Gordon sat three rows from the front, leaning back against the hard church pew as everyone in the congregation welcomed the presenter. Frankly, Owen wasn't happy with her organization one bit. He had a bitter pill in his mouth over the whole orphan train ordeal and wasn't in a mood to listen to her explanation, which he had demanded earlier when he spoke to the pastor in a private conversation.

Cooper Murphy was the owner of Cooper's Ridge as well as the town's pastor. He bought the land, had it platted and leased each building for two years to make sure the recipient followed the rules and regulations of the town's ordinances. After the renter proved he was indeed redeemed, Murphy sold the building for one dollar and the recipient became the new owner to do with the property as they wished. If the owner sold the building, it still had to fall under the town's guidelines. Cooper's Ridge general assembly kept strict rules on this.

Most of the men in Cooper's Ridge were former outlaws of one type or another after they saw the light of their ways. Some men, like Cooper himself, had been heading down a bad road and turned themselves completely around, except polite society wouldn't give them a second chance.

Owen was in that category. He had tried to redeem himself for two years after he accidentally shot and killed a man. Even though it was self defense, he had no witnesses to vouch for him. The only reason he didn't hang was because the town was desperate for a doctor. Even so, every single man and woman in his old hometown reminded him daily how they did him a great favor by not bringing in the hanging judge.

When a traveler visited his office one day he found out about Cooper's Ridge and decided to make the journey to a new life with people who understood what he had gone through. After six months living here, he knew without a doubt this was home. It was the place where he planned to start a family of his own and feel like he belonged somewhere.

Except the woman standing in the front of the church was rambling on about the mistakes made bringing orphans here. "As I said, there was an issue with a few of the children on the Mercy Train. Several of the children did not make it here and we are looking into that as I speak."

Owen, as the new doctor, felt it was his duty to speak for the others as well as himself. He stood out of respect and waited to be addressed.

"Greetings, Doc Owen. How can I help you?"

He nodded. "Greetings, Mrs. Young. I'm afraid that I'm the reason you are having to explain yourself today. I spoke with Pastor Murphy the other day because I had to close my practice early to meet the train in Mill Ridge expecting an orphan and to my surprise there was not one boy on the train. They were all girls and babies."

She nodded. "That's why I am trying to explain what happened. There was a mild disappearance at one of the orphanages we use. While most of the girls and babies came from The Children's Aid Society in New York City, we also were expecting a certain number of boys from the New York Juvenile Asylum."

"What does this have to do with my situation?" Owen didn't mind having to wait, especially since his mail order bride was only due next week, but he had agreed to adopt an orphan boy and wasted a whole day traveling for no reason when there were patients to see. That didn't sit well with him.

"Your situation is a rare one," she told him, smiling apologetically. "Several of the children ran away before the train left the station in New York City and had to be rounded up to travel at a later date."

One of the men in the congregation spoke up. "I don't know why the good doctor wants an orphan! Children who are thrown away are a source of corruption and very few are useful."

Owen turned towards the farmer. He wasn't fond of the man and was glad he only came to town on occasion. "Mr. Anderson, I'm of the mind that anyone can change given the chance. I took in an orphan because they also need a home and I plan to provide for a good one right here in Cooper's Ridge, along with a mail-order bride."

Mr. Anderson snorted. "You'll regret those quick decisions. You just mark my words, Doc. Mark my words."

Olivia Young's voice rose, causing everyone to settle down. Owen glanced her way and realized she was trying to keep order. "I do have some good news for you, Doc Owen. I was waiting to tell you after the service today. Since we are speaking of your situation right now, I'm happy to tell you that a telegram came this morning indicating the child you ordered was found and is being sent here as we speak, along with an agent of the Juvenile Society to make sure he arrives this time. They'll be coming in on next Wednesday's train."

"Thank you, ma'am. I appreciate the update and all you've done to fix things." Owen sat down, not wanting to make a spectacle of himself. After all, she did find the boy. It was an inconvenience since his bride-to-be was coming in on next week's train as well. He had wanted to deal with each one separately in order to get to know them. Now, it looked like they'd be here at the same time.

Owen guessed he was trying to make everything fall into place by having the boy come here first to get to know the town since living in New York City was far different than here. He wanted to give the orphan time to adjust. He should know nothing works out the way it's supposed to.

As far as the mail-order bride, they had conversed in writing several times and felt she was going to be an asset to his family. He'd think about her later. Right now all he wanted was everything to work out the way it was supposed to.

The pastor took his spot in the pulpit. "Thank you, Olivia. I am a believer that we all can make a difference and this mercy train idea has been a positive light for so many families who didn't have children and for those wanting more. In the Bible it clearly states to take care of widows and orphans and I'm proud of the fact that Cooper's Ridge is doing their due diligence. Thank you, Doc Owen, for taking in an orphan, along with a mail-order bride to help grow this town of which I am extremely proud of. Enough said. Let's move on to our morning scripture."

The pastor's voice faded out as Owen sat back in his seat once again, contemplating all he had taken on. When he came to Cooper's Ridge six months ago, Murphy had taken him aside and assured him that he'd be able to buy the building that housed an office and living quarters when his two year period was up.

Owen had signed the lease and opened his practice. The first few weeks had been flooded with patients that hadn't seen a doctor in ages. Some folks in town had to travel into Mill Ridge or Wichita Falls for a doctor and didn't want to go that far, so they suffered without getting the help they needed. Now, everyone who didn't want to travel lined up in front of his office daily.

The practice wasn't making a lot of money but it was enough to pay the lease and have some extra for savings. He supposed when his mail-order bride got here, he'd have to dish out extra money for her clothes and needs as well as the child. Owen didn't mind though, but he knew he'd have to budget the money more. They'd have enough to get by, along with some savings he had from before. The important thing was having his own family.

What he found out pretty fast was not all patients paid with coins. Many of the women brought him so much food he had enough to last a month of Sundays. He was given milk, home-churned butter, fresh baked bread and cakes in lieu of payment and accepted it since most of the folks were also trying to build up their own business and lives.

When they brought him chickens he had to put a stop to those payments. He didn't have time to feed quacking birds and get chased around the yard while gathering eggs. Instead, he asked the owner of the chickens to keep them and bring him a few eggs instead. One middle-aged man looked at him as if he were crazy for refusing such fine birds, but Owen was adamant. He was a busy man.

Once a month he rode to Dallas in a rented buggy for more supplies at the apothecary shop. Luckily for him, he didn't have to send away for what he needed. The Dallas Apothecary had enough supplies to sell him and other smaller offices the important medicines they used in their practices.

While in Dallas, Owen usually spent the night in a hotel, along with a good supper at the hotel's restaurant. It broke up his life and gave him a chance to wear his Sunday best besides church. He assumed when he married his future bride, she'd come along with him. The orphan child, too.

Owen couldn't recall what the pastor preached about since he was too busy daydreaming. When everyone got up, he made his way outside, where the congregation was gathering in the side yard for some pastries and lemonade. Most of the townsfolk and neighbors mingled for an hour or so until they went on their way. The farmers in the area usually hung around longer since Cooper's Ridge was the only town close to their farms. They usually didn't get to mingle much with other people all week long while tending to their land and animals.

Owen was the opposite. He had a thriving business speaking to people on a daily basis. On Sunday, he stayed long enough to grab a pastry he liked before going on his way. It always seemed like the townsfolk wound up asking him medical questions the moment they saw him, so he tried hard to avoid them by leaving early. He needed a break away at times, too.

"Why, Doc Owen! How nice to see you here."

He stuffed a piece of the apple dumpling in his mouth so he wouldn't have to talk. He lifted a hand and waved, looking apologetically at the recipient. Most times, they did all the talking anyway and all he'd have to do is nod. Owen should feel bad but he honestly did not.

"I'm so happy to hear you are taking in one of the orphan children, Doc. My school is filling up rather quickly with our last batch of children and that pleases me immensely."

The teacher of Cooper's Ridge was fairly new. She came out here a few months before Owen had, along with her new husband who ran the gunsmith shop. Molly and Harrison Nelson were from a place called Noel, Kansas and were good friends with Cooper Murphy. They really weren't as bad or talkative as most of his patients.

Owen looked up to find the two of them watching him eat his apple dumpling. He tried to give a smile and another wave. "Excuse me, my mouth is full," he told them both.

"No worries, sir. We'll be on our way while you eat. Have a great day and make sure to come along on your new son's first day of school so I can register him and go over all the details with you."

That's if I ever get an orphan boy! He knew the committee was trying hard to make the Mercy Train work, but if an orphan was running away at every chance he got, Owen honestly wondered if the boy would be more trouble than what it was worth. He finished his apple dumpling and made his way down the street towards the livery. He was going to go on a long ride with his face in the wind, as he contemplated this new life he was about to start.

Cooper's Ridge had been a new start six months ago when he came here not knowing what to expect. Now, he was about to become a husband and father at the same time. Was he worthy of these new titles? He had killed a man and even though he thought he put it in his past, the nagging feeling that always arose when he wanted something more came to the surface.

Was Owen truly worthy enough to have his dreams come true of a family to call his own?

He saddled up the mare at the livery and headed out to open fields, gazing back to find Cooper's Ridge behind him.

With the wind in his face as the mare galloped through the field, he gave a nod to the man upstairs. Guess he'd find out next week if he was worthy or not.

READ THE RUNAWAY ON AMAZON - AVAILABLE TODAY![1] (https://www.amazon.com/ Runaway-Outlaws-Orphans-Coopers-Ridge-ebook/dp/ B09VK7LPRK)

---

1. https://www.amazon.com/Runaway-Outlaws-Orphans-Coopers-Ridge-ebook/dp/B09VK7LPRK

Don't miss out!

Visit the website below and you can sign up to receive emails whenever Cyndi Raye publishes a new book. There's no charge and no obligation.

https://books2read.com/r/B-A-PXQ-FJQEC

BOOKS 2 READ

Connecting independent readers to independent writers.